March 31, 1971

To Bharati and Clark,
On this momentous
occasion, etc—

Paul Friedman

AND IF DEFEATED ALLEGE FRAUD

And If Defeated
Allege Fraud

STORIES BY

PAUL FRIEDMAN

UNIVERSITY OF ILLINOIS PRESS

URBANA, CHICAGO, LONDON

Some of the stories collected here first appeared in the following publications, to whose editors grateful acknowledgment is made for permission to reprint: *Quarterly Review of Literature* ("The Arm of Interchangeable Parts"), *Perspective* ("An Evening of Fun"), *The Arlington Quarterly* ("The Forecast"), *Trace* ("The Alphabet of Mathematics"), *Four Quarters* ("A Matter of Survival"), *New World Writing* ("Never Lose Your Cool"), *New Directions in Prose and Poetry* ("Portrait: My American Man, Fall, 1966" and "The Story of a Story"), and *Quartet* ("An American Memory, 1966").

Several of the stories in this volume were written at Yaddo. I wish to take this opportunity to acknowledge that and express gratitude.

THIS BOOK IS DEDICATED
TO MY MOTHER AND FATHER,
Eva AND *Jack Friedman,*
AND TO MY WIFE AND DAUGHTER,
Mary AND *Mysti Friedman.*

CLAIM EVERYTHING, CONCEDE NOTHING,
AND IF DEFEATED ALLEGE FRAUD.

The Arm of Interchangeable Parts

I

"May not a man have several voices, Robin, as well as two complexions," said his friend.

HAWTHORNE: "MY KINSMAN, MAJOR MOLINEAUX"

THE game was a drag. Unless someone got hot fast, which wouldn't happen, nothing would happen. Nothing would happen. Week in and week out it was the same thing; nothing really could happen. They played five ten and a quarter; the stakes weren't high enough for anything to happen—not with the sort of stunted streaks they could put together—and they weren't going to raise the stakes because this wasn't that sort of game, this was a friendly game.

"Everything ought to be turned inside out, it's all ass backwards."

"That's right, but there's about as much chance of things changing as, oh crap, why aggravate yourself, just accept it, why knock your head against a stone wall?"

"Goddamnit, we ought to change ourselves, you know that?"

"Things keep on getting worse, that's the only kind of change there is."

"No kidding, we ought to change ourselves."

"Great idea, how, take a pill?"

"Sure, why not, they've got pills for everything else."

They played on Thursday nights; had they never missed a Thursday night then, by this time, that in itself might have created some interest, but when something came up they'd call off the game, they had sensible attitudes. "A nickel." They weren't fanatic. From time to time other hands sat in but usually it was only them, two neighbors living in the same building, a four-year-old apartment house across from a new Waldbaum's which didn't make it a spanking suburban shopping center but it was something, it wasn't bad, it wasn't bad if you didn't count traffic which could back up for a block when trucks made deliveries on Avenue D and then not only did traffic stand still but yelling, screaming, cursing, horn pounding, exhaust, air pollution, asthma. "Bump you a dime."

"I've been getting your mail."

"The letters of yours that are addressed to me are dull."

"Don't blame me, I didn't write them."

"How would you do it?"

"What?"

"What we were talking about last week, changing yourself."

"How should I know?"

"You were the one to suggest it, weren't you?"

"Was I? It must have just popped out."

Deal. Bet. Crap.

But it really didn't matter. Change scooped in. Shuffle. C'mon, deal. But it really didn't matter.

Harry turned from the table and pointed out the window at Avenue D and beyond it. "All the crap that goes on out there kills something inside us," he said. "It has to. Crap takes its toll even if you're not being personally crapped on. Take Vietnam: At the very least you have to deaden yourself to keep from losing your appetite."

"Nobody forces you to watch the news while you eat supper."

"That's a very intelligent remark. You're really sharp tonight."

The neighborhood was primarily residential, old one- and two-family frame and brick homes that seemed substantial from outside but with foundations in a state of decay.

"Nobody puts a gun to my head and makes me watch television, that's true, but there are other kinds of pressures at work on us, you know that."

Harry Arm, one of the Thursday night card players, was thought of as an eligible bachelor. He wasn't. Eligible implied good catch; even bachelor sounded romantic, hinted single by choice. Not at all; he wanted wives by the score, especially blonds: honey, platinum, natural, dyed. He guessed he was ugly; he knew he was awkward, knobby.

"How would a man go about changing himself, that's an intriguing idea."

"I've been thinking about it, there's only one way, you'd have to make it a game."

"Why?"

"Otherwise it would seem as if you were working against yourself. It wouldn't be the same as losing weight or learning a foreign language, you know. This would be tampering with something deeper, making it a game avoids that."

"A few minutes ago you were all for it," Harry said, referring to the suggestion made weeks back to change, "what happened?" He felt there was a deeply rooted mean streak in his playing partner.

"Nothing happened, I'm simply looking at it from all angles and pointing out some of the difficulties."

A bank of television monitors operating on closed circuit was in the lobby of the apartment house. About to enter the lobby, a person could scan the screens and see if anyone was lurking inside. The monitors were on a wall opposite the brass colored mail boxes. "What a way to live."

"A little caution never hurt."

"Three kings. I know what you mean, but still . . ."

A generation had passed since Harry had been the age of the neighborhood boys: Now they were long haired, snotty, with Cuban heels, butterfly cuffs, belted vests. And the girls with them, the girls . . .

His parents had come to the neighborhood before the Depression and opened a tailor shop. Eventually it grew to a clothing store; their success was typical: They'd worked hard and seen something come of their work.

Like other neighborhood people, his parents had complained about services received from the city: The sanitation was poor, not enough buses ran on the D line, even the water pressure was low.

They talked about change.

Not long after his parents died Harry moved to the apartment house; the apartment house brought many more people to the immediate neighborhood and parking became impossible. The streets were filthier than before. Oddly, they were also emptier. There had been a gradual change over the years and now there was something new to contend with, fear. People felt uneasy going out at night; they claimed you took your life in your hands if you went down to the corner to buy a paper or across the street to mail a letter. It hadn't been that way when Harry's folks had struggled. People had never before felt it dangerous leaving a front door open to catch an evening breeze.

You can't be too cautious these days, it's a damn shame but that's the way it is; it's becoming a jungle, the neighbors complained, what a way to live.

And the girls . . . The girls were as brazen as the boys.

"Kids get out of school today and they can't even write. Cut."

"We're breeding a generation of idiots."

"It's a national disaster."

"Athletics prepares you for the game of life, wasn't that the pitch your high school coach gave you?" Harry said.

"In certain ways life's a joke."

"You must have been a real all American boy."

"Sometimes I think life's just a goddam joke."

"Well well, am I hearing right? The untapped depths are surfacing."

"Stop sneering for a change, will you?"

"Let me correct one of your earlier statements. I'd have to say life's more a game than a joke. Saying it's a joke places too much emphasis on humor."

"You're such a sarcastic bastard."

"That's because I was never a high school football hero."

"You're involved in a train of conversation that I just don't follow."

"The subject works me up."

"Then get yourself laid."

"Are you trying to redirect my energies?"

"Get yourself some pussy Harry."

"When did that become the issue?"

"When hasn't that been the issue with you?"

"You're a big talker, *Get yourself some pussy Harry,* but for all your loudmouthed talk you're just a timid little man."

"Who are you describing," the big man asked, "me or you?"

"Just look in the mirror, but take my advice, don't be fooled by what you see."

There were different explanations that the neighbors gave for these changed conditions: The country's going down hill;

7

parents don't take an interest in their children any more; it's an outside element coming in. Some blamed it all on the mayor.

The idea of change: Game in, game out. It dragged; it stuck. Pushing it further: If it's a game then how would you play it? Let's be exactly the opposite of the way we normally are. Laughing it off, going ahead, setting up the machinery: How do you decide how you are? One person could decide how the other person was and vice versa. Titillating. It's crazy, stupid— Working out the rules. Once you figured out how the other person was, and when you got the other person to agree, then the opposite would be easy, it would be apparent. And you wouldn't have to check on the other person, he wouldn't cheat, there was no possibility of cheating; cheating would mean not changing yourself and that's the whole idea, that's the whole kick. The only way to win would be to play straight, you'd be cheating yourself if you didn't. What a fantastic aspect: A game where cheating would be self-defeating.

Why not:

Why not: play another game.

Another game.

Another type of game.

A different game.

His partner was named Harry Arm. Amazing, what a coincidence, people said, two Harry Arms. There couldn't be more than two Harry Arms in all of New York and here they both were living in the same building, people marvelled. It's not so surprising, Harry said, there are probably more of us around than you realize.

They realized they couldn't go on this way: only discussing. Lack of action was costing the game its spice; it was losing life being talked to death. Either do it or don't, yes or no, now or never.

The apartment house was full of people who, for safety's sake, locked themselves in daytime and night.

This Harry Arm was some years older than the other; married and a father. His daughter was a senior in high school, blond.

They locked themselves in regardless of time.

It would be exciting to play another type of game.

They had to decide. Nothing exciting ever came in the mail.

Harry was a big man, a big man going soft, sagging. There were jowls. He was now almost a fat man. Harry Arm was a backslapper and a gladhander. At one time he'd been thought of as lively; over the years he'd moved onto boisterousness; it was an evolutionary process with Harry Arm: He was degenerating. It seemed odd that Harry was an accountant.

"I wonder what would happen if we tried."

"What could we lose, it would only be a game."

"True."

Harry came from out of town originally. His father had been a Lion, a Moose and an Elk. His father had sprained an ankle climbing out of a sand trap on a golf course and for the last twenty years of his life he'd used a flat-headed putter as a cane. The other Harry's father, who came from the old country, was not nearly as spry; nevertheless, he'd belonged to a burial society and now reposed in an out-of-state plot.

"My wife's a semi-sexual."

"Here we go back to the locker-room talk. How gross can you get? How can you talk so publicly about such private, intimate things?"

"If you had a wife who only wanted to get laid twice a year you'd talk about it too." After a moment of silence Harry laughed out loud, boisterously. "I'm pulling your leg Harry. You know, teasing."

"Are you sure?"

"Yes."

"Definitely?"

"Yes."

So it was settled. Decided. They would. For one week. For one week, starting tomorrow, they would try to change themselves. It was artificial; it was ridiculous; it was exciting . . .

They put the cards away. They were sitting in the kitchen. The table was formica. They sat in aluminum chairs. The refrigerator had double coppertone doors and they had a new sense about them. There was an automatic ice maker. There was a garbage disposal and a permanent oven built into the wall.

Accountancy was a growing field and an entirely new area, social accounting, was opening up. Harry thought that if only he weren't so nervous about changing horses in midstream he'd enjoy getting into that.

The decision was made. They sat back, then forward. A tension developed as it began sinking in that they were actually about to begin something new, a new way of living. The seriousness they were feeling came as a surprise to them, as did the sense of fear. A kind of removal, a kind of distance set in.

"This is what I came up with," Harry said when he finally began to speak, "You're a bad man, be good. Before you shout at me for that, or get angry, remember you have the right to decide how to be good. I'm not saying that you're all bad, I know you're not, but there is that element in you, it's in all of us I guess, and if you're going to change then why not for the better?"

Harry looked up, nodded. "That's fine," he said. "You're afraid of women, go after women." There was a leer on his face.

"Hey, no, wait a minute, hold on Harry, no sir. The one I gave you is general, it's supposed to be general, that's the whole idea, you better think something else up for me."

Harry frowned and rearranged himself in his chair. "Okay," he said after some time, "you're too restrained, you have to give in to your impulses more. Remember, I'm talking about action, not running at the mouth."

"That's better," Harry said.

"All the way around you have to give in to your impulses more, even in your card playing."

"That's fine. That gives me plenty of leeway," Harry said.

"You're damn right it does. You can't complain about that not being general enough."

"I'm not complaining. I said it's fine, what more do you want me to say?" There was an edge to his voice.

There was a bottle of Seagram's 7 that Harry took out of the kitchen cabinet. It was dangerous, exciting; at this moment they didn't feel protected. Even though they might get hit over the head any time they went into the street, nevertheless their lives had not been dangerous; their lives had been safe. No more, not now.

Checking for mail usually only gave them a chance to watch television a moment.

What a fantastic thing. Two grown men. Playing secrets. They swore. Secrecy. Thrills. They wondered if there were any other people in the building who were feeling the kind of excitement they now felt. It was a sense of life, as if they had raw nerves exposed. What they were experiencing was so unfamiliar, it felt so unreal, that it seemed to them they must be dreaming.

They sat at the table a while longer; then Harry unlocked the door and they said good night wondering what would happen next.

II

"Had Goodman Brown fallen asleep in the forest and only dreamed a wild dream of a witch-meeting?
"Be it so if you will."

HAWTHORNE: "YOUNG GOODMAN BROWN"

The next day, after a difficult morning in the store, Harry told Mr. Simmons, who worked for him, that he didn't feel well, he was going home. Good, Mr. Simmons said, you don't look yourself.

He was going to go after that woman, or, to put it another way, play the game.

Really?

Was he?

Yes.

Definitely.

Acting on impulse, losing restraint, doing what comes naturally.

All day I wait
to masturbate
and nothing comes
but water
cool
clear

water— He laughed. Those days were gone, that was over: He laughed. He didn't need leeway; the hell with leeway.

He knew what he wanted.

It's a treat to beat your meat
on the Mississippi mud:

Crud. That was a thing of the past.

In the elevator.

Go to
fourth floor.
Knock on
big door.
He couldn't believe he was doing this.
He was doing this.
Knocking.
Hearing things.
"Hi."
His cheek twitched; his bowels loosened.
She was at the doorway in capri pants.
The sound he'd heard hadn't been the roaring in his head
but the whirr of her vacuum cleaner. Vacuum cleaner:
housework, housewife, mother: Harry Arm, oh God, what
are you doing here?
"Can I come in?" His voice almost cracked.
She didn't seem suspicious, why should she be? He'd been
a neighbor roughly four years, a friendly neighbor, a fond
neighbor, a neuter neighbor.
"Sure, but the place is a mess. I always clean on Fridays."
Unkempt from the housecleaning, she brushed some hairs
from her face. "Too bad you weren't here a few minutes ago
to give me a hand pushing the furniture around," she
smiled, then turned and started down the hall.
Following.
Heart pounding.
Tension unbearable.
It was unstoppable, no stopping now, momentum had
developed.
Caution to the wind—
Cynthia staring.
Dumbfounded.
Absolute stillness.

Unbelieving.

She thinks I'm dangerous. Crazy. What have I done? What will happen?

This didn't happen.

Hand still out in the guilty position.

"I . . ." he started.

"Yes?"

Silence.

"Harry I think you better leave."

Continued staring. Then she turned and went into the living room.

He stood, frozen. She wants me to follow, he said to himself. Fear; he wanted to leave. He moved forward woodenly and halted at the edge of the living room. He'd already risked everything. Her back was to him but she could see him in the mirror. Connecting a new attachment to the vacuum cleaner, working at it intently, she deliberately ignored him. She might call the police if I stay, he thought, this can't be me.

He was paralyzed in a nightmare, unable to move, not forward into the living room or backward out of the apartment.

Cynthia was vacuuming the cushions on the couch.

"Hi."

Startled.

Diane.

When had she come in?

"Can't you shut that thing off, mom, what a racket." Going past she looked at Harry. "I hate Fridays in this house," she said as she put her school books down on the table and took her coat off.

She'd looked at him meaningfully.

Terrified.

She'd never looked at him that way before.

"Goodbye."

He raced up the stairs.

What had she seen?

What have I done?

Knocking.

"Let me in will you Harry?"

His door wasn't locked.

"Does your mother know you smoke?"

"That isn't all she doesn't know."

This was impossible.

Her blond hair.

It was happening so fast.

Impossible.

His phone.

She got off him and answered.

He knew who was calling; there was no question in his mind.

"Oh, we're having coffee," Diane said.

She hung up.

"Who—?"

"Mom."

"Your—?"

"Yes."

Knock.

Cynthia.

His life was not dragging any more.

"It's quiet downstairs now," Cynthia said. Diane's blouse was half buttoned; Cynthia ignored it. "Isn't that what you wanted, a quiet apartment? Isn't that why you came up here, for quiet? I think you'd better get downstairs now."

"And I suppose you're going to stay," Diane said.

"Yes." She stared at her daughter.

Diane left, slamming out furiously; then Cynthia turned to him, came close. "I'm dissatisfied," she said, melting, "how did you know? Satisfy me."

There.

Closing the door behind her, Harry—alone now—realized there was danger of an explosion; he thought his chest might burst. To relieve some of the pressure he let out great gales of laughter. His wildest dreams were being realized; this was a fairy tale.

I'm a family man, he said to himself, two women from the same family in the same afternoon. Mother and daughter: It was supposed to be a national problem but he personally had just bridged the generation gap. A feeling of light-headedness ran through him; but he also felt strong, stronger than he'd ever felt, strong enough to live forever.

This was only the first day of the game and permanent change had already taken place. He felt like writing the news to people he knew; it was too good to be true.

Harry Arm liked to think of himself as burly, but today that was impossible. He felt gray, overburdened, tired. Last night's excitement had dulled him: He'd twisted, turned and hardly slept at all.

Harry Arm: Be good bad guy, bad guy be good.

He would. He wanted to. I will, he thought, I will. I want to.

Would it be good to set wrong right? Weak would be more like it, he told himself, it would be weak.

He took the bus to the subway, got off the subway at Borough Hall and walked along Court Street until he reached the office building where he worked as an accountant; then the elevator to the seventeenth floor and with only a nod to the girl who worked the switchboard he went to his desk.

If being weak was a fault and fault was bad, then he was bad and he'd be good. That seemed simple, obvious. But those words, You're bad, be good— They were so broad, so open . . .

He'd wronged his wife. It was eating away at him, gnawing at him: The rot was locked in. What did that mean, Be good, you're bad. What exactly did it mean?

He was doing her a disservice: It wasn't an honest relationship. She was entitled to that: honesty. She loved him. It was dishonest and he was to blame. There was only one way to rectify it: tell her the truth: that he didn't love her; she was entitled to that, theoretically.

But she wasn't theory, she was flesh and blood and truth would end the marriage and that was fine for him but after all these years, at this stage of the game, where would that leave her? She'd never had any interest in a career; her home and family were her life; she never looked at another man. So . . . If only he'd argued, fought, but he hadn't, he'd covered up. No one knew anything was wrong, not even Cynthia. What a shock it would be; she'd crumble, crack . . .

He wasn't sure if he could last out the morning. An ugliness had crept into him because of his hollow core; because of the lie at the center of his life he'd surrounded himself with brashness; he used it as a protective covering:

Cynthia was satisfied; he wasn't.

He wasn't a human sacrifice.

She was devoted to him.

He couldn't walk out.

She was entitled to truth from the man she loved. Around

and around it went. He wanted to apply himself but couldn't; the morning dragged. He could no longer remember why he'd married her, but now to keep the marriage going he had to deceive and deception was no basis for marriage. At one time he'd wanted Cynthia badly, he remembered that, but somewhere along the way that had faded, vanished. He wondered what it was like for Cynthia when she caught a sudden glimpse of Diane who now looked exactly as she herself had once looked. That had to arouse difficult feelings, he thought; when she saw Diane she saw what she no longer was.

He made an excuse and left the office early to go to lunch. Don't be foolish, he told himself; he couldn't; he wouldn't: Not for any game. Make the best of things, you're a family man, you have a fine family. Diane was no longer a child but it would still be difficult for her. Furthermore, even if he did leave he probably wouldn't be able to live with himself because of the guilt he'd feel.

No answers; hazy; unclear; confusing; dark; unreal, his life. Its secrets. He was not eating. Seeing where he was—on the subway platform going home—he realized a momentum had been developed that couldn't be stopped and when it came right down to it if anything was a game it was his marriage, his marriage was the game, not this, so . . . He was wide awake. So many times he'd dreamed of this: Sudden action. Spur of the moment. On the bus, off. Into the building.

Not checking the monitor.

Past the mail.

Walking up the flights instead of waiting for the elevator. Breathing heavily: weight.

Unlock door.

Forcing himself.

In.

Further.

All the way.

Empty.

He stood in the center of the living room.

Nothing.

This was impossible. Unfair.

Unreal. How could this be?

"Hi."

Startled.

Diane.

When had she come in?

Disheveled.

"From upstairs," she said.

He looked at his daughter and saw his wife.

Blouse half buttoned.

Disheveled.

Cynthia.

He was on the roof. Something had happened. What was he doing on the roof? He'd been driven to the roof. He'd gone up the stairs, unlocked his door, empty, then—

What had happened?

Everything clear.

He could see clearly from up here. No walls. No obstructions; only the wire mesh that surrounded the incinerator. He'd seen clearly: Everything inside out. Almost dizzy. This was impossible, none of this was happening. Moving toward the edge of the roof. He was afraid.

He couldn't remember. What had happened?

Perspiring heavily.

Pull yourself together, concentrate: No aerials on the roof because the lease didn't allow that; he was an accountant; it was a game: You're bad, be good; worried about hurting

Diane and Cynthia; everything reversed: You're good, be bad; it wasn't a game, not a matter of hurting them, it dealt with hurting himself. No. That was crazy, sick.

Stop. It was sexual, demonic. He felt the wind. This was wrong, this urge. Where was caution? Closer; he couldn't stop. There was no guard rail or protective wall at the edge. It was exciting because of the danger, that was the thrill; the excitement was real, alive. He was taut; he felt each inch under him. The danger. One slip— He moved closer.

Into the apartment. Something had happened.

Everything reversed.

At the edge now. Almost swaying.

The roof of a seven-storey building.

You'll lose balance.

Don't look. Pull self back. This was wrong; too dangerous. Protect yourself.

Then he tried to backstep and couldn't. He was unable to move away from the edge.

Startled. Stunned. How could this be? This was a nightmare: alarm; confusion. Don't panic. What was going on? Try to hold on, concentrate: Civil and tribal wars were raging in several African countries. There was an urge in him, under his skin, almost like a tickle, to go another step; it made him want to laugh; he felt light-headed: that last inch which would take him over the edge to nothing and emptiness.

Bits of paper and pieces of soot caught in the wind whirled about him. The Middle East was in turmoil and in Cyprus— Reversals: Another inch would take him to the very center, to everything.

He'd reached the roof by opening a massive steel fireproof door. Greek Cypriots— His knees wobbly, throat parched; this was unreal. No one was going to come running up here to save him, to drag him to safety. He had to think, he had to get hold of himself, save himself. Turkish Cypriots— I have to, he said, oh God I have to. Nerves tingling. The temptation to give in, let loose— Open up, unlock, let the rot out. He was going to die; he was right next to death. He almost cried. The lie at the center of his life—he tried to calm himself— that's why he was here, in this danger—because of the lie— was, was: that he lied to himself. He blurted it out; he trembled. That was the central truth of his life: not to others, to himself. Everything upside down. It wasn't that he deceived Cynthia, he deceived himself, to protect himself.

Everything inside out: He hadn't crumbled, cracked . . . Still standing.

The way to win would be to play straight, you'd be cheating yourself if you didn't.

He felt himself calming. Perhaps it was his imagination but he thought the air was clearing. He wondered if he could go now, turn away, turn back, get off the roof, return to the safety of the apartment—

The apartment—shock ran through him—this deceiving, this self-deception: He was still doing it. Tell the truth, face it; spell it out exactly: What had he seen in the apartment?

He could barely breathe. He was yanking and twisting to wrench himself free. It was a moment of hysteria.

The most dangerous thing to do at this height was look down. Harry's eyes dropped while he was battling wildly at the edge; it was accidental.

Before he realized what he was doing—looking—he saw Harry Arm clearly. There were no walls and no obstructions.

He stopped struggling: It was as if a cord had been cut or a nerve severed.

After all the struggling at the edge, now there was quiet and stillness. That man had been with his wife, that's what he'd seen in the apartment, that's what he'd faced in the apartment, that's what he'd run from. He'd seen his own worst fears confirmed. The struggle was over. There was no dizziness. He was still looking: Harry was carrying an envelope in his hand. Harry Arm had been with his daughter, that's what he'd run from.

It was out. There was no furor; he didn't feel faint. On the sidewalk, standing still, he saw that Harry, looking jaunty and sure of himself, had a grin on his face. He could walk away now, he was certain of that; he was free to leave the edge. He didn't want to injure or hurt himself. He wanted to smash Harry Arm; he had reason. He wasn't thinking of Diane or Cynthia, this had nothing to do with them.

The way to win would be to play straight, that meant honestly. You'd be cheating yourself if you didn't. What kind of game was this where, according to the rules which he himself had made up, he was a winner? He must have won. What was the prize?

Harry was underneath; he didn't lose his balance; rather, he took a final step sending himself over the edge and down with a murderous force. They came together; the two became indistinguishable, melted into one, into nothing.

An Evening of Fun

The Fein family owned a dog, Spot, a mutt. Over the years they'd grown attached to him and when it became clear that he was no longer as young as he once had been, when after walking him for a few blocks he'd start to lag behind and mope instead of run ahead, they decided to take him to the vet for a checkup. According to the vet there was nothing much the matter with Spot; he gave the dog a shot, some iron pills, and that was all. The Feins noticed that in filling out Spot's chart, under Approximate Age the vet wrote: Six Years Old.

When the dog had followed their son, Harold, home from third grade he certainly hadn't been a pup; they'd guessed him, then, to be about four years old, and that had been six years ago; that would make him ten now. The Feins didn't mention this to the vet and outside his office they were overjoyed: A dog Spot's age would have many healthy years left.

Two years later the Feins had to have Spot put to sleep; it was a sad occasion for them; it was just like losing a member of the family, they said.

Sarah Fein sat over her cup of morning coffee staring off into space: Harold, he'd announced a decision: marriage.

24

The girl wasn't Jewish. They'd discussed it calmly but what was there to discuss? Many young people did it today, Mrs. Fein knew that, it was a common thing. Harold had told her a month ago and since then she'd lived with it.

Mrs. Fein had made her son promise one thing: that he wouldn't get married until he was done with his studies. That was still a year and a half away, but Harold was no baby. He was twenty-three, two and a half years in school already, and three years in the army. He was a man.

Harold had promised that he and Gail, the Gentile girl he'd met at his midwestern college, who came from a small town in Wisconsin and lived on a farm, would not marry until a year from June. That was the way they'd planned it, he said, letting his mother know that he was not giving in to her, their plans happened to coincide.

Mrs. Fein was thinking there were many good reasons why they shouldn't marry:

The difference in religion: Marriage was hard under the best of circumstances, why make it harder, why look for trouble?

Today young people entered into marriage too lightly. It was as if marriage was something to be tried on for size and if it was too tight in the crotch or pinched under the armpits, then—

What about children? Before they're born you can be very liberal about what religion you're going to raise them, but afterward it becomes another matter. You'll let them choose —fine, when they're adults they'll choose; until then you have to choose for them, that's what parents are for.

Mr. Fein had died of a heart attack five years ago, not long after Harold had gone into the service. The owner of a small plumbing supply company, he'd left some savings, there was money from closing out the business, insurance. . . . Mrs.

Fein immediately sold the house in East Flatbush and moved to a small place on Ocean Avenue.

After getting settled there she'd caught the full brunt of everything: Loneliness: husband dead, son gone—Time: so much of it, how to handle it? A son, a husband, a house—that had taken her time. Her life had suddenly emptied and she needed to fill it again. The thought that at her age, when time was beginning to run out, she had to start killing time: waiting for Harold's letters, his furloughs, his calls: that was unbearable. A life of her own was necessary, outside interests.

Harold was going to bring her home from college during the Easter break so they could meet. But she was sure he had chosen a nice girl, that wasn't the question.

Something was crowding its way into Mrs. Fein's mind. She frowned, concentrated, then realized it was her own image intruding, being reflected by the toaster on the table. Her face was squeezed together, elongated, like a turnip.

She nibbled at the toast but it was stiff now, and cold. She held the toast between her fingers: dark brown toast with bits of black to it, and her fingernails tinted neutral, shining.

It was Mrs. Fein's special gift that she could accept her years; no battling Time with eyeshadow, sunlamps, diet. She grew plumper, softer, grayer, and made no foolish attempts to remain girlish; she wore looser clothes, not tighter brighter ones like some women. She was a reasonable woman.

Why look for trouble?

But it wasn't a question of *looking for,* Gail existed, she'd already been found. Mrs. Fein wanted only what was best for her son. She again became aware of the distortion and saw how hideous she could be made to look. A turnip. She changed her position. There were harder marriages than

this, ones where there was a large age gap between the partners, ones where people of different races marry, she kept telling herself that, but, finally, she couldn't see what that had to do with her son's marriage.

She was looking at it realistically, sensibly.

A well preserved woman of fifty-three certainly appeared more attractive than a gawdy battered looking one who might pass for forty-nine. And there was no pouring herself into tight pants, no gold-spangled, high-heeled, open-toed shoes: what torture. Wrinkles just don't smooth out, you can't get blood from a stone. She gracefully accepted age and seemed serene because of it.

Eventually she found an outside interest, made a life: volunteer work, fund raising. For medical research, particularly the heart. Its diseases had to be investigated, conquered, cured. Cerebral palsy, cancer, all illness had to be fought. She licked envelopes, rang doorbells, went to dinners. Because of her busy afternoons she had to rush through the mornings and at night she was tired from a full day.

But that wasn't enough; she'd filled her day but it wasn't enough. What she did on the outside, publicly, was fine, it took up her time meaningfully, however, if on the inside, privately, she were to lose her son, it would all become meaningless. Again and again, during the last month, she'd thought, Why look for trouble—

The telephone rang.

Mrs. Fein wasn't sure if that thought, if those words were meant as advice for Harold or herself.

"Hello?"

"Sarah, this is Della."

"Della, how are you?" The excitement was immediate in Mrs. Fein's voice.

For a moment words jumbled out: I've been meaning to call you, how is everything, what's new— Mrs. Fein blurting all that out in one long breath, stopping only when she ran out of breath, laughing, adding,

"Hold on a minute Della." She went to turn down the stove.

There was a nice morning sun, Mrs. Fein opened the curtain to get it.

These two women, friends even before their marriage, their friendship going all the way back to the days when both had done clerical work for A. Selig, Inc., Importer-Exporter, had, over the last few years, allowed themselves to lose contact with each other. After marrying, they'd lived within walking distance in East Flatbush. Then, when Henry and Della Simmons moved to an apartment near Prospect Park, they saw each other less frequently but always on special occasions: anniversaries, children's birthday parties, New Year's Eve. Harold, twelve, enjoyed visiting the Simmons' because of their fourteen-year-old, David, who even as a youngster had been thoughtful and attentive. David would take him across to the park, let Harold put on his spiked shoes, and bat long flies out to him. Later, when David was sixteen and his sister, Beverly, seventeen, the Simmonses moved to Manhattan and it became a special occasion any time the families managed to get together. It was because of Beverly that the Simmonses moved. Not that they ever said so in so many words, but it was clear. Their Manhattan apartment wasn't as spacious as the one in Brooklyn, and it was twice as expensive, but it was a much better address, there was a doorman, that sort of thing. It was more desirable, somehow, that Beverly live in that kind of place.

Over the years the couples had seen less and less of each other, but they never said at the end of an evening together, "We'll have to do this more often," because they knew they wouldn't, the words would have been false, and there was nothing false in the feelings they held toward each other.

When was the last time they'd visited? Before Joe had died, was that possible? That long ago? They'd surely talked on the phone since then. When was the last time for that? A year? Two? More?

"Della, my God, how long has it been since we've gotten together?"

There was a sound from the other end of the line, muffled.

"What?" Mrs. Fein said.

No response.

"Della," she asked, "are you there?"

"Yes."

Mrs. Fein waited. Nothing else. That was strange.

"How's Henry?" Mrs. Fein asked.

"Henry's fine," she answered.

Henry: quiet, good natured, he loved exercising, he was always wanting to show you the palm of his right hand, callused from handball. That Henry, of so many years ago, lean, tan, no longer existed, Mrs. Fein realized. He's probably bald now, and paunchy . . . Time.

"And Dave, my God, how old is he? Twenty-four, twenty-five now? What's he doing?"

"He's twenty-five. Dave's fine." Her voice was tense. "He moved, he has an apartment right near us, you know."

"How wonderful."

"Yes, he's a real comfort."

There was a rattle from the front door and mail fell through the slot. Mrs. Fein, with the receiver at her ear, walked toward the kitchen doorway in an effort to see if any of the letters were from Harold.

From the other end of the line, silence. The silence was ominous.

"Della, is there anything wrong?"

There was no answer.

Mrs. Fein ran out of telephone cord and strained to see. She said, "It's quiet here for me. You know Harold's away at school." She paused; Della didn't comment. "How's Beverly?"

There was glossy paper with multicolored printing on it: advertisements for detergents, and free coupons, pennies off.

She was getting frightened. "Della, what's wrong, what's the matter?"

"My daughter isn't with us any more."

There was no letter today, it seemed.

Mrs. Fein knew that Beverly had remarried several years ago, the remark didn't make— A deep sob came over the phone.

"Della," Mrs. Fein yelled; "Della," she screamed into the phone.

Now there was no sidestepping it, the meaning was clear.

The sobbing stopped and in a tiny, pleading voice Della said, "Yes?"

But there was nothing to say. Della was pleading for words that would help. Mrs. Fein was terrified: There were no words. . . . "Della, get hold of yourself, please." She saw her fingers turning white as she clutched the receiver. "Don't talk now, you're too upset, I'll call back later, hang up."

She could hear the terrible breathing on the other end. Della was going to speak.

"Beverly's dead. Last year. She took her own life," Della said, before breaking down completely.

"Della," Mrs. Fein screamed into the phone, "hang up, I'll call you back later, I promise, hang up."

There was a click.

Dead?

A person's daughter, her friend's—killing herself: She felt woozy, frightened, overwhelmed.

Mrs. Fein was afraid to call back, afraid of hearing that unbearable groan of loss again. Too upset to do anything today, she called the Medical Research Foundation office, explained that she wasn't feeling well and wouldn't be in this afternoon. Then she sat down, stared at her wedding photograph on the mantel, and next to it a photograph of her son, a picture of him about five years old sitting on a merry-go-round riding a horse with a cowboy hat on and a look of pure enchantment on his face, and she cried for everything that had past.

Joe was dead. The full force of that hit her again and she couldn't believe it. Her husband: she'd never see him again; gone, dead, forever. She cried, cried until finally by repeating those words, He's gone, dead, forever, they lost their meaning and her mind wandered:

To that other call from Della, years ago, years ago but like yesterday, the call that had come not long after Beverly's first marriage, a marriage the Simmonses had not been at all happy about.

Mr. Fein had been in poor health—he'd just come out of the hospital after his second attack. And it was under the guise of that—doctors—that the telephone conversation worked its way around to—Della stopped hemming and hawing and— The long and the short of it was: Beverly needed an abortion, they were looking for a doctor.

Mrs. Fein couldn't believe her ears.

—And they thought that maybe, since she and Joe were having so much to do with doctors lately, they might know one who—

An abortion? She's married.

It would be annulled.

Mrs. Fein was stunned. She'd never heard of such a thing.

Live long enough you see everything, Della said.

They didn't know any abortionists.

Della kept right on talking and it became clear to Mrs. Fein that asking for a doctor's name was just an excuse, Della was calling to get this off her chest, she had to tell someone.

The only reason Beverly got married in the first place was because she and Henry were against the boy, Della said. Contrariness; being stubborn. The boy hadn't gone to college. A girl who has everything, who's nineteen, who could get anyone, does this girl quit school to run away and get married? To a boy she's known three months? It was ridiculous. They'd met Arnold only once during that time. Frail, pale, nervous. Picked at his food and ate like an ant. No wonder she hid him from us, meeting him downstairs, downtown—

Good manners, polite, he had money, he was wealthy, that wasn't the question. To just get a rich boy, that wasn't why they'd done all that they'd done for Beverly. What does he do, this Arnold? His father owns a chain of dry goods stores. That's nice for his father, but what's Arnold do? As many times as they asked that the only answer they ever got was: His father owns a chain of dry goods stores.

They eloped.

But the abortion, the annullment, what about that, Mrs. Fein asked.

Today she comes in, married two months, announces she's pregnant, sits down and cries. Henry's at work. You're sure you're pregnant? Yes, I just came from the doctor. I'm having a hard time, Arnold's strange. Nineteen, the world at her feet, she had to get married. He's got a peter, what's so strange about him? He's strange, he's not the way I thought he'd be. Did I tell you to run away and get married, did I force you, did I break your arm? She stops crying and now she's looking at me in a funny way, like she's up to something. Don't you want to know why he didn't go to college, why he wasn't working, why he won't come here and visit? Why? He's afraid of you and Dad. He made me promise I'd never tell this, but it doesn't matter now, we're married, what difference can it make? He made you promise you'd never tell what?

He has a history of mental disorder.

Oh my God.

Well don't get so upset, he's not a raving lunatic.

I'm calling your father, don't move.

For God's sake you're acting just the way Arnold said you would.

This is what you had to get involved with?

She started to whimper. Arnold can't live without me. He needs me. He said if you knew you wouldn't understand, you'd split us up. He was right.

Needs you? He needs trained professional care.

Oh stop it. He's been well for two years, he's all over that problem. He's wonderful, he's the most wonderful person I—

Henry came right home.

Why are you telling this to us now, he asked.

She couldn't answer. I don't know. She cried. You're my parents, who else should I go to? I want you to tell me what to do. I'm afraid. I don't want this baby.

Now you come to us?

Oh God, what's going to happen to me. I'm afraid.

Headstrong: she's finding out life's no game.

Henry called the lawyer.

There's grounds for annullment if one partner conceals a disorder of that nature from the other partner.

But he didn't conceal it, I knew. I knew.

You make a mistake you have to pay, nothing comes free.

Okay, I'll do it, okay, just don't make me go back, I can't face him. Let me stay here. He's so delicate, oh God, what will this do to him?

That's that, she's in bed, we gave her a sleeping pill. Now we need a doctor.

That call was carved in Mrs. Fein's memory, forever.

The rest of the story had come in dribs and drabs over the years. Arnold didn't fight the annullment. Beverly lived at home. Time passed. She moved from one job to another, tried school, travel. Nothing seemed to take. Then, suddenly, she met a wonderful man, got married. He was older, divorced, perhaps not what the Simmonses might have at one time wanted for Beverly, but that didn't matter now. He was very good to her, he loved her very much and the Simmonses were happy.

Everything seemed to be looking up.

Now this.

Mrs. Fein sat in her kitchen staring at the telephone. She dreaded making this call. She and Della hadn't just fallen out of touch, admit it, they'd been avoiding each other, that was the truth, and it could all be traced right back to that abortion call: Della had bared too much, it was dirty, she hadn't confided, she'd confessed. It was a confession. Mrs. Fein had tried to blot it from her mind, but she couldn't, it was engraved, forever. And she was sure Della knew that.

She stared at the phone.

She wasn't going to call back.

It was all so ugly.

It showed what was possible.

She didn't want to know, not the details.

How ugly.

She sat in her chair and her mind was definitely made up: She wasn't making this call.

A sound, she jumped, the phone, oh God, Della—then she dropped back in her chair because it was a horn blowing not the phone ringing— But it could have been!

Della could phone her, she'd forgotten that. Della might call, Della could call. She might be dialing right now.

It was late winter and the trees were bare. On the sidestreets off Ocean Avenue there were one-family frame houses set well back from the sidewalk leaving plenty of space for gardens and lawns.

For a winter sky it was exceptionally light. There were few clouds, no gray. A sun. No cutting wind or raw dampness. The weather didn't fit. Rushing from her home, no destination in mind, away from the phone, Mrs. Fein left Ocean Avenue and turned down streets she wasn't familiar with—the more unfamiliar the better, the further from home the better: She wanted to lose herself. And in the middle of a strange block she noticed a house that was just about falling apart: It was happening all over. The call was out of her mind, she had the willpower to do that. The house stuck out like a sore thumb. Since she was out she ought to do some marketing. What a pity, to let a neighborhood like this start to rundown. The idea slipped away. It was the end of February, Harold should have been a February baby but he'd been a week late, March 2. A battered station wagon was parked in front of the house, with its rear end bashed in. That hardly mattered now, twenty-three years later.

The neighbors shouldn't allow this. It was terrible. In mixed marriages it wasn't only white parents who objected, Negro parents also wanted their children to marry their own kind. What sort of people could live here? Her mother, Harold said, taught in Sunday school.

Mrs. Fein walked slowly now.

She wasn't going to call back. The front door opened and a man came out, rough and ready looking, and instead of going down the stairs he stopped on the top step and started yelling at the little boy who was sitting in the yard, digging.

This kind of weather was tricky, it was easy to catch cold.

A woman rushed to the front door, bleached blond. They were arguing. The voices got louder.

"I'll be goddamned if he's gonna do that," the man yelled.

"Just try and stop him. Keep digging, Jimmy."

The woman wasn't afraid. She was in a cheap kimono.

The little boy had a pail and shovel, the kind children use at the beach. He stared up at his parents.

"Put that goddam shovel down."

She was past the house. The poor little child, not knowing what to do, parents screaming at him . . . A neighbor across the street went inside after emptying garbage.

No one cared.

"Like shit you're boss," the woman yelled.

The door slammed. There was a scream. Mrs. Fein turned. Another scream. The garden was empty. The mother hadn't slammed out of the house to pull her husband off her child, her husband had slammed in after her.

—Weren't supposed to interfere, didn't want to get involved, this type of person, that little boy, she wished she were home, what did she know about this kind of stuff, these kinds of people? Because you want the winter to be over on a late winter day when the sun comes out you fool yourself into dressing too lightly and then catch a cold which can ruin your spring, sick: A little boy sitting on steps sucking a thumb watching his father beat his mother through the door that had banged open. She ran from it:

Home:

Put the key in the lock and heard the telephone ring. Oh no, not now, please, wait. Let me rest first. This wasn't fair, she wasn't ready. Later. It was so loud. She couldn't just let it ring. The ringing. Her head was splitting. She rushed to the phone. Raised it.

A buzz: dialtone. She sobbed.

Mrs. Fein had her things off and she was weak to the point of exhaustion, about to drop. The phone rang. She jumped, ran:

"Yes?"

"Mrs. Fein, are you all right?" It was a deep male voice.

The feeling of relief was so great on hearing Mr. Thompson's voice—her boss at the office—that she suddenly felt lightheaded and giddy.

"I called before, there was no answer. I understand you're not feeling well, what's the matter?"

She had to bite to keep from laughing.

"Mrs. Fein?"

"Yes, I'm okay, nothing's the matter, just a little headache. I just stepped outside for some fresh air."

"You sure? Don't come in until you're all better, you understand that?"

"All right Mr. Thompson."

"I don't want you taking any chances."

"All right Mr. Thompson." She had the laughter under control.

There was silence. Mrs. Fein was sure he'd say something else; Mr. Thompson never liked being all business, especially with the volunteer staff; he believed in the personal touch.

"By the way, how's Harold, hear from him lately?"

"A few days ago."

"Kids," Mr. Thompson said. "They're all the same. Think mine's any better? I got one who's been in Texas for two years and I can count on the fingers of one hand the letters I've gotten from him. He says he doesn't like to write letters."

"Well, Harold's really pretty good about writing."

"Ah, what are you going to do?" he sighed. "Well, take care Mrs. Fein."

"Thanks for calling."

Mrs. Fein dialed Della's number; after all these years she still remembered it by heart.

Della didn't make any reference to the earlier conversation, she had herself in hand. This call was very brief. Della said she'd just talked with Henry who'd suggested that she, Sarah, might want to come over for the evening, about eight, it would be fun, could she make it?

Yes, see you then.

It was an old-fashioned lobby, high-ceilinged, with ornate decorations and deep colors; there were gilded couches, heavy drapes, a thick rug thinning in spots—all this dimly lit. This was the sort of apartment house where elevator operators had not been replaced by self-service elevators; the operators were old and didn't wait patiently in the elevator but paced from the side corridor on the first floor, where the elevators sat when they weren't in use, to the lobby, and when they saw someone standing in front of the directory they'd come over and ask, in a bossy way, who the person was looking for; then, without telling him what floor his party was on, lead him to the elevator and, still wordlessly, take him up, not minding in the least being rude, having been with this house so long that they felt superior to anyone who was merely a visitor.

Whisked to the fourth floor in this way, Mrs. Fein had the last apartment on the left pointed out to her. Before she moved more than a few steps a young man came toward her. "Mrs. Fein, hello, I'm Dave, remember me?"

"David, certainly, how are you?"

They grasped hands. He smiled and led her to the leather bench near the elevator.

There were ashtrays three feet high and full of sand on either side of the bench.

He'd filled out beautifully. Harold was shorter and stockier, both were broad and athletic looking, but where Harold came straight down from the shoulders to the waist, David tapered; they were both very handsome.

"It was good of you to come tonight, Mrs. Fein," David said, drumming his fingers on the bench.

It was a nervous situation. But what a gentleman he'd turned out to be, Mrs. Fein thought. So mature.

"You're the first person they're seeing since it happened. Socially I mean, not business or family. They've just about cut themselves off completely, especially Mom."

"What a tragedy."

"They're starting to get over it now, I hope. I've been telling them that you've got to go on living, you can't just wall yourself in, but Mom, I don't know, she's taken this very hard. Dad too. I tell them they've got to stop blaming themselves, it isn't fair, not to them, and really, not even to Bev."

Mrs. Fein nodded in agreement. Twenty-five years old. She wasn't sure what he meant by that last remark, but it sounded like a healthy attitude.

"It's natural for them to do that though," Mrs. Fein said.

"It's not a natural situation, Mrs. Fein: your daughter killing herself." Then, more softly, he added, "Anyhow, I wanted to catch you before you went in, just to, I don't know, prepare you . . ."

Taking this responsibility on himself: to catch her before she went in, to explain . . . "Don't worry." She patted David's hand. "You're a good boy, David. They can be proud of you." She sighed. "Such sad, horrible things happen to people."

They got up to go but neither seemed anxious. Mrs. Fein suddenly felt very close to David and wanted to ask him about Beverly: Why? Why had she done it?

"David, what was Arnold like?" The words jumped out and surprised her.

"You mean Robert? I never cared for him. No, that's not fair. He's sober, dull, a real Rock of Gibralter—there, that's not all negative, is it? He loved Bev, I don't mean to say—"

"No, Arnold, the first husband."

"Oh, that's funny. Arnold, I really liked him. He was different, that's what got Bev, I think. Not at all modern. Competition, pressure, he couldn't stand that. He was gentle. You don't think of a guy twenty as gentle or kind, even if he is—but that's the way you thought about him. He was wild, too, in his own sort of way; he loved fun: dancing, masquerades, that kind of fun—not football.

"Once we went to Macy's together, this was right after they were married and he wanted to get Bev some kind of wacky surprise, like an automatic toothbrush, just something funny. The store was jammed, it was lunch hour, people were pushing and shoving, it was hectic. Someone gave Arnold a tremendous shove because he was moving so slowly. A little old lady, and when she rushed past him she she had a vicious look on her face and she said, 'What're you, a millionaire or something?' It ruined his day." David slowed down, seemed to be thinking. "He didn't fit in, he felt out of place. He wasn't angry at the old lady, he felt sorry for her . . ." David's voice trailed off.

After a moment, Mrs. Fein asked, "What happened to him?"

David's voice snapped back with a terrible bitterness. "What happened to Bev, that's the real question, isn't it?" For a moment he stared at Mrs. Fein brutally.

Then he laughed.

"Strange, Bev thought it would kill him—what she did: the annullment, or, at least, literally drive him nuts." David's eyes were on the iron arrow which pointed to the floor the elevator was on. "There wasn't a word from him for years. Then, two years after she married Robert, I was with her at the airport, Robert was going away on a business trip and who do we bump into? Arnold.

"Coming back from vacation, Miami Beach. The Fountainbleau, or maybe it was the Caribbean somewhere, it doesn't matter. Tan, healthy, he looked great. Robust. He had a wife, he was snapping his fingers, giving orders, shouting at his kids, he had two children, calling for a redcap, ordering a cab—the whole works. A real man of the world,"

David said. There was a long silence. "A real man of the world."

Mrs. Fein knew she had to say something. "He doesn't sound like the same man."

"That's right Mrs. Fein, you're so right." He smiled at her and the smile frightened her.

She made a move toward the apartment but David didn't follow.

"I guess it was quite a relief to Beverly," she said.

"That he was so healthy, that he hadn't cracked?" There was a fierce irony in his tone and Mrs. Fein knew it, but she didn't know what to do with it.

"Yes," she said.

"In case you're wondering, when they spoke it was only for a moment, Hello, Goodbye." David smiled. "They didn't have much to talk about, you see." He looked disfigured, though no scar showed.

There was a complete change of face. "Hello, anyone home, company's here," David called as if this were a gay occasion. He'd just opened the door. "Here, let me take your coat, Mrs. Fein."

The foyer led into the living room where the Simmones had an elaborate setup that immediately proved useless: the coffee table with tiny sandwiches, the drinks, Henry standing beside the bar, the lacquered look of Gracious Host on his face, Della arranged on the couch in comfort: that whole false front went down the drain when Mrs. Fein's eyes met Della's and simultaneously they started to cry, then rushed across the room toward each other, arms outstretched, embracing.

Henry's expression changed, the bags rolled out and only the hurt showed, he dropped into a gray lounge chair and sat with his hands on his knees, a look of dumb pain on his face; he stared at his wife who was sobbing in the middle of the room, looked helplessly at his son, and finally, futilely, down at his own clenched hands.

David went to the bar and mixed a drink.

The Simmonses had wanted so much for Beverly: When Della had been out of school for twenty-five years, during a winter that was cold and nasty, she took a night course in French at N.Y.U.: She didn't want to hold her daughter back. In her mid forties, she'd had her front teeth capped. It closed the gaps and helped her appearance.

Mr. Simmons, a furrier, worked long, worked hard, made a great deal of money and spared nothing for Beverly.

It was warm in the room, hot, oppressive. Mrs. Fein knew she wouldn't say a word about it, she'd just sit and suffer.

"Did you two meet outside?" Della asked, turning from Mrs. Fein to her son, sniffling.

David nodded yes, anxiety on his face.

"He's such a wonderful son," Della said, turning back to Mrs. Fein.

Mrs. Fein looked to David. He smiled, raised his glass, toasted her and drank.

Della's tear-filled blue eyes, open, pleading, showed her misery, but there were no other indications; she looked very smart in her black cocktail dress with the single strand of pearls and her figure was still trim. Only the eyes . . .

The heat was unbearable. She suddenly became aware of the great silence in the room. How could they stand it?

"You're looking very well," Della said.

It stayed silent. Weren't they bothered by this? Didn't they feel it?

"Did you have any trouble finding a place to park?" Della asked.

Or was she the only one? Was she crazy?

"Maybe you'd like something to eat?" Della asked.

"No, someone pulled out just as I drove up," Mrs. Fein said.

That little boy, what would happen to him with parents like that?

"Sit down."

The mother wasn't any better than the father.

"Sit anywhere."

Henry got up. He sighed heavily and walked toward Mrs. Fein. He nodded his head up and down as he held her eye: I know, I know, you don't have to say it . . .

How the man had aged, not just weight, although he had a belly now, and not the baldness, although he'd lost most of his hair, but the way he was carrying himself, his posture, stooped . . .

There were beads of sweat on Henry's brow; it was hot. She wasn't crazy.

"Just make yourself comfortable," Della said.

Mrs. Fein stared straight ahead, at the painting on the wall.

Henry kissed her cheek. She wiped her cheek. She wanted to wash up.

"Did you decide yet? What can I get for you?"

Henry said, "Della, Sarah doesn't . . ."

"Yes Henry, yes? Can I get you something? What do you want?"

"No, Della . . . Why don't you sit down? When Sarah wants something she'll tell us. Or she can get it herself, it's right over there. That's all right with you, isn't it Sarah, we don't have to treat you like a guest, do we?"

"All right, if you say so Henry," Della said. "Where should I sit?"

Henry was quiet while she smiled at him with her bright, wide open eyes.

"What's the matter Henry, did I say something wrong?"

"No Della. Why don't you just sit where you want to sit?"

"You'll have to excuse us, Sarah, we're not used to company. It's a compliment, really, that we're bickering right here in front of you."

"We're not bickering Della, I just want you to sit down. Relax."

"We are too bickering, Henry, don't say we're not, that's silly. It's a normal thing, lots of married couples bicker, don't be ashamed. Sarah's one of the family."

What a terrible thing for a child to witness, one parent beating another.

David wandered into the kitchen with his drink.

Mrs. Fein sat very still.

"I'm trying not to say anything wrong, Henry. Am I doing all right? Henry gave me very careful instructions about that. Henry wanted me to call you, he says it's important that we begin to live normally again."

On the fingers of one hand. How many letters could that be? Of course, it was an exaggeration, that was just an expression.

David wandered back in and he'd left his glass in the kitchen. "By the way, any time you need the bathroom it's—" and he pointed down the hall.

"Thank you, I think I'll—excuse me." Mrs. Fein got up to leave the room.

David fixed another drink. They watched. Children go so far away, Texas.

"Well," David said, "maybe I'll leave you folks alone for a while . . ."

There was just a slight hesitation, like the sudden taking in of breath, before his parents said, Certainly, of course.

"Have a good time . . ."

"Run along . . ."

"Nice meeting you again, David," Mrs. Fein said.

David gave her a last, imploring look: Remember, they're in no condition . . .

The door closed behind him.

It got very stiff in the room. Everyone smiled. There was a moment's reprive when the light bulb in the end table blew. Henry put in another bulb; it worked. They smiled.

It was silent. They all started to speak, they all stopped. It was tense: Beverly, Beverly . . .

"What's David doing these days?" Mrs. Fein asked.

They jumped on that. "Dave?"

"He's on Wall Street."

"He works for a brokerage firm, Lansing and Co."

It was silent. It was so difficult, avoiding Beverly.

"That's nice," Mrs. Fein said.

"Dave's not crazy about it, actually."

"You know how it is on Wall Street."

"How about some Cherry Heering?"

"If it's a good year they get a very nice bonus."

"Very substantial. Otherwise . . ."

"With Dave it's not just the money though."

"No, that's true, with him it's not really the money."

There was a silence.

It was so hard, getting started on Beverly.

"The bonus is an important part of the salary on Wall Street, that's a tradition . . ."

Silence.

"This was a good year, wasn't it?" Mrs. Fein asked.

Her words sounded in the room. She felt her face go red. "For the market I mean . . ." She stopped, it was clear, she didn't have to explain, or blush. The girl was dead. Every word couldn't be weighed, you couldn't measure every phrase. It had been a good year, for Wall Street.

"I'm glad Della called you," Henry finally said. "We've been thinking about this for a long time." He looked at Mrs. Fein meaningfully; Della got up from the sofa and walked to Henry's chair; she stood beside him and held his hand, she seemed composed. "I don't know how much Della told you this morning but Bev wasn't sick when she died, she, she—"

"I know, Della told me," Mrs. Fein said. There. It was out. "I was shocked, stunned—" She stopped speaking, words were inadequate.

And she had the urge, sitting there about to listen to them talk of their dead daughter, to tell them of some great sadness of her own, for their sake, but, thank God, there was nothing in her life to match this.

"The maid found her."

This had to be gone through. Like sick people on the mend, the Simmonses had to show their scars. They recalled details and incidents.

Beverly, after the first marriage, had tried her hand at decorating; she'd even been involved with an art gallery for a while; she floated from one interest to another.

Robert was wonderful through it all—he'd stayed calm, made the funeral arrangements, taken care of the details.

You never met him. Such a strong person.

Their daughter had grown so far away from them.

Mrs. Fein felt a pounding in her head, probably the cordial.

"Robert had his feet on the ground."

To have to go through this with everyone, explaining, explaining . . .

They felt they no longer had the right to interfere in Bev's life. But it was terrible, watching her suffer, watching her life waste away. They were afraid to say anything, they'd said too much already. The girl was so cold, she held them at such a distance.

"—so patient with Bev and her ways. So understanding. Robert has no family. I guess we're like family to him. We still see each other."

Cold as she was toward them, far apart as they were, until she married Robert Bev did not move out of their apartment.

In her mind's eye, Mrs. Fein had not pictured the Simmonses as sick people with scars to show, but, rather, as people in mourning. She'd half expected them to be unkempt, Henry with stubble on his face, bleary eyed, Della pale, plodding around the house in slippers. But there was Henry, at his fourth-story window looking out across the river toward the Jersey palisades, sipping Scotch.

You do what you have to do.

The carpet was eggshell, an impossible shade to keep clean; it was spotless and this added a sense of luxury. At the end of the foyer there was a mirrored panel of wall and right in front of it was an end table holding a piece of sculpture, metal of some kind, black and twisted, like the branches of a crippled tree. There were three modern paintings on the wall. Mrs. Fein sensed Beverly's influence in this apartment, she'd definitely left her mark.

"Let's face it," Della said, "she panicked and came running home and we made her do what we wanted instead of what was best for her, it's that simple, don't you think, Henry?"

"Well, I'll say one thing, after it was all over we felt guilty and that's why we were afraid to speak to her."

"You'd think," Della said, "that parents would want what's best for their children. But no, you have dreams and plans for them, so you fool yourself into believing that what you want for them is best, not what they want."

"Of course, Della," Henry said, "I've said this before and I'll say it again: She didn't want to be pregnant. She wanted that abortion, we didn't force that abortion on her."

"Didn't we?"

"Absolutely not."

"It was our job to straighten her out, Henry, not take advantage of her. That's what we did, we took advantage of her."

"Okay, let's forget the abortion," he said. "Why did she marry Arnold, that's the question."

"I don't know, maybe you have a point, maybe we didn't take advantage of her, it's hard to say."

"Why did she marry Arnold?" Henry asked again.

"Don't start in with me about that," Della said hotly. "I'm trying not to say anything wrong."

"You think she married him just because we said no?"

"Why then?"

"Maybe she loved him."

"Love?"

"Love. Infatuated, I don't know. Maybe she loved him, yes."

"Who? Her? Miss Iceberg? Miss Saltpeter 1956?"

"Don't talk about her like that, in such a dirty way."

"I'll talk about her any way I want, she's my daughter."

"That's right, she's your daughter, you ought to be ashamed of yourself for God's sake."

"I am."

That stopped them cold. Those words were so sudden, so unexpected, spoken so softly.

Della finally said, "Don't worry about this Sarah. This is how we nourish ourselves, we eat off each other. It keeps us alive, it's all we have left."

Henry said nothing, he stared at his wife.

"If talk could bring her back don't you think I'd change the way I talk?" Della yelled.

She cried.

"Could you turn down the heat, I don't know what's the matter with me," Mrs. Fein said, "but I suddenly feel so warm." She was growing faint.

"Are you feeling okay?"

"Yes, fine, it's just so warm—maybe if I could have a cold drink."

They turned down the thermostat.

Mrs. Fein remembered Harold saying Reform Jews accepted intermarriage way back at the turn of the century. This was not a new thing. In fact, there wasn't much difference between Reform Jews and Unitarians, Harold said.

Mrs. Fein hadn't meant to ask anything of the Simmonses, she didn't want to impose on them, they were the sufferers.

The school had an excellent history department, Harold said. This was one of the main reasons he'd chosen that university. And he'd be in every Christmas, plus summers . . .

To have to go through this with everyone, explaining, explaining . . .

There were lots of New Yorkers out there. It wasn't uncommon at all for New Yorkers to go that far for a good education, people told her.

One thousand miles from home.

Joe had been a great believer in education. He would have approved, she told herself.

If that's what you want, okay. You're sure you don't mind, Mom? Mind what? Being alone. I'm not alone, I have you. Harold flushed.

You do what you have to do.

Thanks Mom, thanks a million.

"Talk dirty. You're a fine one to bring that up," Della said. "You were the one, Henry, who thought that she got married because she was pregnant, you thought she had to get married."

"I thought that? You're imagining things." Henry turned to Mrs. Fein.

Mrs. Fein held the cold glass in her hand and it helped. She touched it to her face.

"Don't listen to her, she doesn't know what she's saying," Henry said.

What did that girl let him do to her?

"You must have thought she was a real hot little number, your daughter," Della said.

"This has affected her mind," Henry said. "She's imagining things. Just listen to this."

"I guess I'm imagining what you said to her that day when she came and told us she was pregnant. What you said to that girl was brutal, absolutely brutal."

Henry stared at his fists on his knees.

The lights. She'd forgotten to turn the car lights off. The car might not start. Mrs. Fein didn't want to get stuck here.

"Remember what you said? 'There's still time for a doctor and lawyer to get you out of this mess.' Well, well Henry?"

"I don't deny it," he said without looking up.

"That poor girl. Nineteen. What's so unnatural about a nineteen-year-old who's upset about being pregnant?

They're upset for a while, they cry, then nine months later they have beautiful children," Della said.

Mrs. Fein started toward the window but stopped in front of one of the paintings: D. Simmons it was signed.

"What we did to that poor girl," Della said.

David, an artist? Mrs. Fein moved around the room and saw that the other two paintings were his also.

"David did these?" she asked.

"He paints," Della said.

Silence.

"They're nice, aren't they?" Della asked.

Triangles, rectangles, squares. Blue green yellow.

"Yes."

"He's a serious minded boy," Henry said. "It's nothing, it's a hobby."

"Don't say that," Della said. "Why do you discourage his painting?"

"Discourage? Who's discouraging him? I'll let him paint, in fact I'll buy him paint: buckets, gallons, whole drums full. I'll get him brushes too, and if brushes are old-fashioned I'll get him rollers. If he wants to paint, Della, he'll paint, and if he doesn't want to he won't. It's him not me." He turned to Mrs. Fein. "Dave doesn't paint any more."

Della picked up the telephone.

"What are you doing?" Henry asked sharply.

She hesitated. "I was going to give Dave a call."

"Leave him alone," Henry said. "For God's sake, one night let him—"

She held the receiver but made no move to dial.

Silence.

"I thought he was going out," Mrs. Fein said.

"Who, Dave, going out?" Henry laughed. "You know what

his good time is? Sitting home in his apartment waiting for her to call."

"He's a son, he cares for us."

"She tell you he lives around here? Around here: one flight below."

"He wanted to, you know that," Della said.

"Sure I know that," Henry said sarcastically, "he loves us. Della, he's a grown man for God's sake, he has his own life to live. Let go of him."

Della seemed discouraged, without strength. She hung up, looked away from her husband and toward Mrs. Fein. "Dave feels he has to, I don't know, look after us. Maybe Henry's right, maybe I shouldn't be so dependent on him." Her eyes were on the floor.

The girl who got Harold would be a very lucky girl. He wasn't artistic, but he was good with his hands, he was handy. To have a man like that around, these days, with the price you had to pay for labor, that was worth anything.

"Harold and David ought to get together," Mrs. Fein said. "He's in history, you know, and he has tentative plans to go on to law school."

"Cold," Della suddenly yelled at her husband, "like a statue. You don't know. That girl was torturing me by staying here, getting even. Why else do you think she stayed all those years, for the view? Wake up. You went to work everyday, you weren't around here with her all day long, you don't know what she was like. She was getting revenge. She hated me."

Henry didn't speak and Della turned to Mrs. Fein. Now her voice was on a frighteningly steady level.

"Robert was leaving on one of his trips and she took him to the airport. They'd been married two years. David was along and they were coming here afterward for supper. Accidentally she ran into Arnold at the airport. He was happy, with a family—a wife, children—what could she think? How she must have hated us!"

Henry spoke up. "She couldn't have children. We didn't know that. We didn't find it out until after, after she died." He was staring at the paintings. "It was because of the abortion . . ."

"When she got here I could see something was wrong, but I thought she was upset because Robert had just left again and she was going to be alone. It broke my heart to see her that way.

"God forgive me, even though she was my own daughter we didn't have the kind of relationship where I felt I could say anything personal to her. But this time she looked so sad, so heartbroken, that I took her aside after we ate and I said, 'Bev, isn't it time you started a family?'"

"You didn't know, Della," Henry said, "don't blame yourself."

"The look that girl gave me, I can't describe it. There was a little smile on her lips. Henry, I swear, it was pure hatred. My God, there's just no other way to describe it."

"We did what we thought was best," Henry said.

Mrs. Fein was sure she'd caught a cold during the morning.

"She should have told us," Henry said.

"It was her fault, right Henry, the whole thing."

Henry didn't answer.

She was starting to feel a stiff neck.

Mrs. Fein's head felt too heavy to hold up. Della was looking at her, so deeply, so openly: Mrs. Fein felt she should confess something.

"I think I'm getting a stiff neck."

"What?"

"Nothing. Nothing, it's just the position I'm in."

"The next day she went to a doctor for an examination," Henry said. "He said, No children, definitely. She went home to her empty walls and killed herself."

"It was an overdose of sleeping pills."

"The maid found her."

Mrs. Fein said, "I remember you said that before."

Mrs. Fein did not get home until late. David came back before she left the Simmonses' apartment.

After letting himself into the apartment with his key, David bumped into the end table and shook the sculpture. His face broke into a wide grin and he tipped an imaginary hat as his parents and Mrs. Fein turned around.

"Hi," he said, and he went directly to the bar, weaving a bit.

The Simmonses nodded hello, exchanged a look with each other and, communicating silently, decided to act as if nothing were wrong, go about their business as usual: discussing Beverly.

They had only half a mind on the conversation; the thread of the conversation had been lost and Della picked it up anywhere.

"Love?" Della said. "She was inhuman, she couldn't love."

"That isn't why Robert travelled and you know it," Henry answered mechanically, as if speaking from a memorized script. "He did plenty of travelling before he married Bev.

Robert enjoyed being with her. Dave," he said, unable to restrain himself, "did you go out?"

"Mom been saying that Robert travelled to get away from hardhearted Beverly? She been saying that again?" David asked, lounging against the bar. He laughed. "Did I go out? I'm back aren't I? That means I had to go out doesn't it, how else could I come back?"

They laughed at David's words, trying to make the words funny, and they sneaked little looks at Mrs. Fein.

"I know it? Don't tell me what I know. I know my daughter's dead"—Della was peeking at David, watching him refill—"that's what I know, that's all I know. Wouldn't you like something to eat, Dave?" she asked. "Can I get you a sandwich and some coffee, we're going to have our coffee now."

"Coffee shit. Why did she marry Robert, that's interesting question."

In fact, Harold said, Unitarianism interested him.

What a situation that would be: left with a dead battery late in the night. I think I'd better run downstairs and see if I left my lights on.

"Robert loved her, he was good to her, kind, gentle . . ."

Climb into the car. Turn on the ignition. It starts.

"Beverly wanted to get married, to try and lead a normal life. He offered her that opportunity . . ."

Stop daydreaming. Wake up. The lights are off.

"Excuse me," David said as he burst out laughing, "excuse me but you two make me want to puke."

"Stop it! Stop it! You don't know what you're saying."

"She tell you why Bev stayed here?" David asked Mrs. Fein. "Just to torture her—pretty crummy of Bev to do a thing like that, don't you think, huh Mrs. Fein? Or, how about this, you get this routine? One says, We did what we thought was best. The other says, We interfered. Other says, We guided. The other says, We fooled ourselves. Other says, We loved—"

"Being drunk doesn't give you the right to say such horrible things," Della shouted, and she started to cry.

"I believe I may have had a bit too much to drink tonight," David began in a ridiculing tone, "but—"

"*David!*" Henry screamed.

Della's sobbing continued.

David quieted. The snottiness left him and suddenly, as his mother huddled on the couch and cried pitifully, he began, "I'm sorry, I'm sorry, I didn't mean that, please. You know I didn't mean any of that." He seemed very sober now. "Please Mother, I'm sorry, really."

Della looked up, blinked, stared at him, and tried to smile. She stood, "I'll make coffee."

"I think I better go wash up," David said, and left the room.

Henry walked to the window. He sighed. "He's had so much responsibility this last year that sometimes, once in a while, it's understandable, he goes on a binge. I don't mean a drinking binge, I mean he just lets himself go, says anything, the craziest things you can think of."

Della stepped into the room. "You don't know what it's been for him Sarah. He gave us so much strength. We, we sapped him. This sort of thing, this kind of outburst, don't judge him by it. He's been a fountain of strength."

"Serene?" Mrs Fein repeated, surprised.

"Yes," Della said, "and you'll never know how I envied you that."

Della had cleared the coffee table of the sandwiches which had turned stale and set out Swiss cheese, dip, crackers, and there was jam and butter and hot rolls and bread, the coffee was black and strong and Mrs. Fein found an appetite.

"And I thought you called, I don't know, because we were friends, old friends."

"Yes, but mainly because you seemed serene, as if you'd made peace with yourself. It's hard to explain, but both of us felt that way."

Henry nodded in agreement.

"Well, anyhow, I don't get paid, it's strictly voluntary."

"It must be very fulfilling, knowing that you're doing some good."

"The money's for heart disease mostly, that's my main interest. Of course, there's the personal interest, you know, what with Joe . . ."

"I think that's wonderful, the world could use more people like you."

"More people would do this sort of work if they could," Mrs. Fein said. "I believe that. I guess I always think the best of people—after all, I see them giving, being generous, donating . . . And remember, I'm lucky I can afford to do volunteer work, most people can't. If Joe hadn't left me relatively well off . . ."

"Still and all, not everyone would do it."

This was much better. And the Simmonses had shown their scars, they'd be better off for it. Mrs. Fein felt a certain sense of satisfaction.

"There's a lot of office work involved, just filing and that sort of mechanical, monotonous work. Also, making telephone calls, selling raffles, getting things typed up . . .

"Jerry Lewis is very good with cerebral palsy. There's a Mrs. Steinmetz in our office who's very involved with that. I think it was in her family."

"I agree with Mom and Dad, Mrs. Fein. I think it's a

wonderful thing, your doing this. In more ways than one. I mean, I think it keeps you alive, keeps you young, rather than just sitting around the house, you know, not doing much."

"It's true," Mrs. Fein agreed, "you have to do something, otherwise . . ."

"I mean that's the problem with so many men who retire," David said, "they just sit around the house and they sort of go to pot."

"I understand that you're working on Wall Street now," Mrs. Fein said.

"Yeah, I'm Robert's office boy."

"David, don't say that, it's not funny," Della said.

The Simmonses blushed and looked quickly, guiltily at Mrs. Fein.

"Funny? It's pathetic," David said.

This was endless, endless, a cesspool.

The Simmonses were falling over each other speaking at the same time.

"Robert thought—"

"That is, he felt—"

"You know, Harold's enlisting was a great blow to Joe," Mrs. Fein said dully.

"A lot of people feel working for a relative is the hardest sort of work."

Mrs. Fein wondered if her nose was running. She brushed her upper lip and nostril with her finger and her finger came away dry. "He knew that his father was a sick man."

"Especially in the world of finance no one does anyone any favors, it's all strictly business."

"It wasn't any surprise to me, Joe's last attack. You wouldn't have been surprised either if you'd seen the aggravation Harold's joining the army gave him . . ."

It was endless. It was not words, it was noise. It was a cesspool.

Mrs. Fein had made an excuse, left. It was a blur in her mind. She'd had to get out of there. She didn't want to know. She didn't need the details. Had it all been a lie? Couldn't he even hold a job?

Things hadn't always been this way. Was it just that she was getting older? She'd often heard older people say, Young people these days don't seem to have fun any more, they don't know how to enjoy themselves. That was silly. That statement, she'd always thought, told more about the person speaking than it did about the younger generation.

This wasn't the same thing, was it? Things really hadn't been this way years ago, had they? Suicide; drinking. Maybe he was just a glorified office boy, maybe that's all he could do. Working for his brother-in-law at a make-believe job. Maybe he lived one flight below his parents because they had to take care of him. It was all so ugly.

Houses had been kept up. People cared. They took pride. Foul language had been kept off the street.

Maybe he'd start painting again, his triangles, his circles.

It was all so complicated now, so different. She'd learned so much tonight; it had been an education. Maybe she just wasn't modern. Maybe today it was considered smart for a woman to use four-letter words in public, for a son to swear at his parents, for parents to lie about their children . . .

If that's the way this world was now then she wasn't sorry at all that her life wasn't beginning now, that, if anything, it was moving toward its end.

This wasn't the world she knew, the world she cared about.

Lying in bed, at home, staring into the darkness, she heard the normal sounds that a room makes: squeaks, noises, and somehow they frightened her, she felt out of place, a stranger here, although this room had been her room for five years.

Unitarian: A person who believes God exists as one being in opposition to the doctrine of the Trinity. Unitarians accept the moral teachings of Jesus but don't believe he was divine. That was the definition. She wasn't even sure what it all meant. Was that a Christian or wasn't it?

Harold, would he be a Jew or a Unitarian? If he were a Unitarian could he be a Jew, too, like a vegetarian?

How complicated, how complicated and ugly it had all become.

And she couldn't help thinking, in that bed, alone, the one she'd never shared with her husband, Joe, with whom she'd shared bed for thirty years, she couldn't help thinking about the dog, Spot, and their feeling for him, how pure and simple and truthful it had been.

If only everything could be that way.

The Forecast

"It's funny that CBS would build a TV studio here in this neighborhood," the son said.

"Now when firemen come tearing down the block you don't know if it's a false alarm, a real fire, or a prop for some TV program," the father said.

"You ought to buy stock in CBS pop," the son teased. "With a studio right on the corner you could keep an eye on your investment."

"When I want to throw money away I'll give it to the ponies."

After eating lightly they'd gone to the front porch to sit; the father did his own cooking now.

"I wouldn't be a fireman today for all the money in the world," the father said. "Bricks are thrown at them, rocks, bottles, why should they put up with that?"

"That's not the case around here though, is it?"

The father ignored that and sat silently.

The son continued: "By and large this is still a nice neighborhood pop, stable."

"Listen, you're not safe anywhere today."

They were sitting in aluminum chairs with interlaced plastic strips of green and white. Easy and light, the father found them manageable; he had four of these chairs and he kept them stacked in the front hall, two against the wall, two behind the door.

"Wait and see, one of these days firemen are going to wise up and walk off the job."

From habit now, when a car parked on the street the father would openly lean forward in his chair to see who got out.

"I wonder why CBS put a studio here," the son said.

"As a matter of fact I heard Howard Hughes was interested in that corner."

"What? You must be kidding."

"No, you ought to come around more often."

"What reason could Howard Hughes possibly have for—"

"Who knows? Believe me now at night you can get hit over the head here on 47th Street almost as easily as you can in Red Hook. Things change. Maybe from a certain point of view it's a highly desirable location."

"Even in better days it never was highly desirable pop, let's not go overboard."

It was 7:30 in the evening, the middle of June. Gnats were out. The air was heavy. Primarily a residential area, the houses were old, one-family, frame. For the six-story apartment house to be built on the corner, for the studio to be built across from it, to get the necessary changes in the zoning regulations, palms had been greased.

The houses were semi-detached.

"Hello Mr. Stiles."

"Hello Billy."

The neatly dressed fourteen-year-old blond boy waved and smiled and without stopping ran down the porch steps to the sidewalk. There was a cement divider between houses.

"Who's that pop?"

"Remember Cooper? He moved to Phoenix last year and sold the house. You never met these new people. Billy's their oldest son. This kid's always looking for odd jobs to pick up a little extra money, he's got it in his head he's going to pay for his own college education."

"Good luck."

"Look, it's nice to see a boy who's willing to shoulder responsibility these days. That's not a common trait with young people any more."

The son shifted on the green and white. "Wasn't there a law passed saying municipal employees couldn't strike?"

"That won't matter," the father said, "they'll get around it."

A Good Humor truck with two American flags mounted on top was rolling slowly down the block. The studio's side wall was on 47th Street: long, flat, windowless, the only break in its cement surface was the locked gunmetal gray rear exit. Billy and his friends lounged along the wall.

"There are laws against everything," the father said. "Law doesn't seem to mean much any more."

Across from the studio, looking like an apartment house doorman in his brown uniform with gold stripe and piping, was a security guard who stood duty in front of the apartment house from early evening until the following morning. The gutter was busted.

"Forty years ago a man making twenty-five dollars a week lived better than a man today who makes five times that salary."

"That's irrelevant."

"That's irrelevant. Whatever I have to say is irrelevant.

You don't know how good the times were back then; today no one's happy."

"It's irrelevant so far as it doesn't have to do with the particular point I was making."

There was a junked car on the street two houses down. A wrecker had been towing it; the towline snapped when the driver hit a pothole. The wrecker pushed the car to the curb and left it. "If you're talking about money you have to come to grips with inflation." The engine was gone, the tires were gone. Windows had been knocked out, glass was scattered in the street. "A man on a pension, a man living on a fixed income, don't tell him that salaries are going up."

"I'll grant you that, no one's denying that, that's obvious."

"And those people who *are* making good money, so what? Don't give me any phony statistics about how many washing machines they have. Washing machines are no index of being happy. I'm sure most divorced couples had excellent washing machines."

"Pop what's that got to do with what I've been saying?"

There was a vague odor hanging in the air; other neighborhoods had a certain sewer odor, here a hint of smoke hung in the air.

Billy's friends finished their ice cream and, making sure not to clog the sidewalk, leaving room for people to pass, played ball against the studio wall.

The Good Humor truck crossed the avenue and its bells faded. There was a loose ball; the security guard tossed it to Billy. The sound of a siren could be heard, faintly, then closer, louder. A red car with a cherry light flashing raced down the block and pulled to the curb at the corner. The father stood and watched. The boys moved off. Fire officials got out. There were more sirens and a fire truck came down the block; it was followed by a second. Children raced after the trucks. As the firemen jumped off their trucks the children climbed on and swarmed over the second one until finally they sat in the driver's seat on top, rang the fire bell in front and chinned from a ladder where the ladder extended over the street.

Billy came rushing up the stairs.

"What's on fire?"

Billy stopped. "I'm not sure Mr. Stiles," he said and though he was in a great hurry he waited until he saw he was not going to be asked another question before rushing into the house. Moments later he came out holding some sort of small dark object in his hand which looked like it could be a pistol.

People inside the apartment house were standing at their windows. Their behavior was calm; they were watching. There was no sign from the studio that it was involved.

Firemen were milling aimlessly. "It's nothing," said the father, "another false alarm." Billy, with his friends, was now standing at the foot of an alley midway between the fire trucks and the porch. The firemen began to chase the children off the trucks. Parents came from porches to round up their children.

"You know, a person used to get a stiff fine for turning in a false alarm. For one thing it costs the city money to send those trucks out. For another a fireman can get killed rushing to answer the alarm. If I was a fireman—" He cut himself off. "Firemen are going to stop answering alarms, that's what'll happen."

Billy pulled the side pocket of his pants inside out, took a penknife and cut it; then he slit the inside seam of his pants at the upper thigh so that now if he put his hand in his pocket it could go clear through.

"Be realistic pop, they can't. Who'd put out—"

"No one, that's the point." The official fire car took off. The junked car was an eyesore. "I don't get it, what's he doing?"

"Who?"

As a knot of people returning from the corner was passing the alley, Billy ran out at them. He ran awkwardly with a hand in his pocket. "Fire!" his friends screamed, "fire." The people, mostly parents with children, startled, stopped. The fire trucks were just now leaving. "Fire." And then they saw what they took to be Billy's exposed penis sticking out; it was the gray barrel of his pistol sticking out at his crotch.

"Fire!" Billy began squeezing the trigger, shooting at people. They screamed, ran wildly; it was madness. It was confusion. It was a water pistol. For the children, who could tell they were being shot at, not pissed on, it was a frenzy of horror and delight. The adults pleaded, begged, ran hysterically, Billy chasing them into gardens, behind cars, upstairs, flying, screaming, veering off, going straight at one like a bat, swerving, stopping, starting. "He's putting out the fire," his friends were screaming, "that's the hose." They grabbed their sides and laughed till they fell; people on the porches looked at each other, that was all. His friends dropped in the alley from laughter. "Billy the fireman." The pistol seemed endlessly loaded. The whole thing lasted only a minute or so. Billy stopped from exhaustion and barely managed to drag himself back to the alley.

The people were gone; the street was empty. It was very quiet on the street.

There was a front garden below the porch; most of the hedges were broken, the bushes were thick. There seemed no path or direction. Broken bottles and cans were covered by overgrown bushes.

"I'm fit pop, no complaints," Joe answered. "Nothing I can't handle, anyway."

"There's so much violence in the air. Everyday it's something else and it's always the same damn thing, violence. I don't get it." Sparks were shooting from the incinerator. "What about you Joe?"

"I told you pop I'm fine, no complaints."

"There's no one special yet? You're not getting any younger. Do you give any thought to getting married?"

"Marriage, who knows? It's a gamble."

"I won't push but it's nice to have someone in your later years."

"The market can give you a steady eight percent return on your investment if you buy a good conservative stock."

The father listened.

"Buy low and sell high pop, not that there isn't more to it than that, there is, but essentially that's it."

The father listened.

"It's the market that's made America great pop, never forget that."

Billy was coming up the stairs; the father turned. "Why did you do that?"

"Oh, we were just fooling around."

The sound of Billy's friends' voices was in the air.

"Ruining a pair of pants, you call that fooling around?"

"Excuse me Mr. Stiles, I think my mother's calling me."

"And frightening the wits out of people. I thought you wanted to save money—you won't do that by ruining pants."

"Thanks Mr. Stiles," he said, and opened the screen door and went in.

Joe checked his watch.

"How are things pop?"

"Oh," the father said, "so so. Frankly Joe, I stain my underpants."

"So? So what? That's no crime. You stain your underpants. It's understandable. I'm a young man and I do it. In fact, who doesn't? You look great."

"You can't get them clean after a while. I do my washing at the laundromat. People see me folding up the stuff. Things slip my mind," he said, "I must be getting old."

It was becoming difficult; there was a closeness in the air.

"What are you talking about, I forget names all the time. Taxes are stiff but I can't complain, you make do in other words. That's a liability in my line, too, forgetting names, and yet I do it."

"Sorry to hear that Joe but don't kid yourself, there's a difference between a weak memory like yours and hardening of the arteries. Don't run from the truth, you youngsters these days seem inclined to do that."

"That's not fair pop, I'm willing to face—"

The screen door slammed.

"Your mother's letting you out again," the father said, "I'm surprised."

"Hello Mr. Stiles." Billy paused. "There's some kind of new low or bad high forming. I just heard it on the radio. People are worried." His hair was neatly combed. He was wearing a different pair of pants and he waved and ran down the stairs.

A car went past; the father watched, leaned back. "I went back to the place last week Joe," he said, "the boys gave me some welcome."

Joe wiped his arm. "God it's— Someone ought to develop some kind of industrial praying mantis or lady bug that would go around eating all this crap"—he waved at the air in general—"that's messing us up." Particles of soot were clinging to their skin. "Wouldn't that be something, how would you like to have controlling stock in the firm that manufactures that bug?"

"I was really surprised at the welcome they gave me: Where you been, how you doing, heard you had an operation last winter." He coughed. "They found out about that because some investigator from the union was around. I suppose because of all the medical bills the union's been paying. They miss me."

Sparks were shooting from the incinerator against the sky.

"That's one thing, they always treated me well. It's a good feeling to know you're respected, that's something."

The street lights came on.

"Stay away from the glamor stocks Joe, do me that favor. Brustein played the market and he said that's the one thing he learned, stay away from the glamor stocks."

"Brustein, Jesus, that brings back old times. I haven't thought of him in years." He wiped his forehead, there was a smear. "Chrysler's been going up for over a year now. In my estimation it's a good substantial stock and it's going to continue to climb. That's a good tip pop, you could do worse than invest a little in Chrysler."

"The boys asked for you. They all wanted to know how you were doing."

"I'm just fine pop, no complaints."

"You don't have any special girl friend you're seeing?"

"The whole field pop, they're all special to me."

"It's almost seven years since I retired."

"Seven years already, Jesus, that's hard to believe."

"Mom's been gone five years," he said.

Joe didn't answer.

"They all wanted to know what retirement's like. I told them the truth, I told them that sometimes an individual day might drag, sometimes an individual morning might seem like a month to me, but these seven years, looking back, they just flew by. Things have been humming right along for me Joe. They all wanted to be remembered Joe, they remember you."

"Nature's really great the way it makes things work out, isn't it pop?" the son said. There was a certain tightness in his face.

"I don't want you to worry about me Joe, everything's fine with me," the father said.

"Well," Joe said, "I guess I better . . ."

He'd parked the car around the corner on the avenue.

"You want a cup of coffee?" the father asked.

"No pop, really, it's getting late."

The son stood.

The father rubbed his eyes; they were red and stinging as if he'd been too close to fire. Something was clouding the street lights.

"I'll walk you to the corner," the father said. He locked the front door and said he'd bring the chairs in when he came back.

They went down the stairs. The houses were old and wooden.

They walked silently; there was nothing left to say. It was sweltering. There was nothing left to say. The evening had ended, it was over.

Gusts of black smoke came pouring from the roof of the apartment house.

It was smoldering out.

As they came to the studio wall the rear exit opened. "My God, they just shot the CBS weatherman," a stunned voice cried out. "I think he's dead."

"They, who, get hold of—"

"Some crazy man, I don't know, some—"

"Hello Mr. Stiles," Billy said.

"They've killed him." Was this real. "People said this would happen." It was a groan. "My God, right after the forecast, he was still on the air."

They coughed. There was crying. They turned around. It was smoldering.

Bits of charred paper were scattering in the air.

No flames. There was a great wailing in the street. People in the apartment house were framed in their windows. They were in grotesque positions framed in their windows, arms thrown out, pleading, clawing.

Billy's friends at the corner were singing in eerie high pitched voices.

Many people watched the forecast. A shooting had taken place on television; the weatherman had been assassinated. There were no firemen. There was no net.

Smoke was billowing out.

"I'll get my pistol Mr. Stiles," Billy said, "maybe that will do some good."

The security guard was there in gold braid.

"They kept on telling him this would happen. He wouldn't stop. He said he knew there was danger but he wouldn't quit. They couldn't shut him up, they just couldn't—my God."

A television camera was at the rear exit now, focused on the apartment house.

Billy dropped to a knee, raised an arm, sighted, fired. People threw themselves away from windows and then an instant later they were back, clawing, shrieking, as if flames were lapping at them from behind, as if they were caught in a crossfire.

It was hard to breathe; it was getting harder to breathe. Soot the size of snowflakes was floating in the air. The air was unbearable.

It was dark. Billy was squeezing the trigger. The forecaster, it seemed, was dead. A camera was capturing it all. Joe was in the gutter. The father fell in darkness. "I don't live around here," Joe said, but his voice was lost in song.

The Alphabet of Mathematics

THE post office opened its doors at 9:00 A.M. and closed them at 4:45. Located on the basement level of the Empire State Building, a sense of official drabness hung in the air. Ball-point pens were chained to writing tables; criminals' mug shots were posted on walls and clerks' faces appeared from behind barred windows. What little relief there was came from brightly colored recruiting posters.

Mr. Long, the foreman, whispered an inspector had been nosing around. The clerks grumbled. Unreasonable fear went through Mott; his fingers trembled. While it was understandable that an inspector's presence might make a clerk uncomfortable, there was nothing especially unusual in an inspector nosing around. Why was he so frightened, Mott wondered, he was sure he'd done nothing wrong.

Later, Mott cut his coffee break short; something was compelling him to balance. He'd been on the job more than thirty years and this was the first time he'd ever suffered that urge. When the foreman came over at 3:30 wanting to know why his window was still closed, the clerk lied and said a customer had come back complaining she'd been short changed, he had no choice, he had to balance.

Long shook his head in disgust. Mott was the best window man here. "Dealing with the public's the hardest job in the world," Long said.

Mott nodded. Long was new. Foremen became foremen in the post office because of political pull. After clerks worked their way to the position of foreman, particularly while they were still greenhorns, they tended to side with the customer: the customer's right, don't argue with the customer, don't offend the customer . . . Ordinarily the clerk would have had to admit that Long was okay, but not this time; this time he was disconcerted, he wasn't balancing out.

Sitting in a cage, thin and bald, with the window closed, on what looked like a dunce's stool, hunched over the counter, touching the tip of his sharpened lead pencil with his tongue as he checked off the figures on his balance sheet, Mott added things up.

"Take you off the window for fifteen minutes and look what happens," Long said, "the lines are out to the street."

Mott didn't respond. A pat on the back from a boss was usually followed by a knife in the back. He could handle as many customers as any two other clerks. Empire State was a Class A station; firms were dealt with that purchased hundreds of dollars of stamps daily; a clerk might take in thousands of dollars a day. That was responsibility. Confidence was necessary. The minute a window man lost his confidence, Mott believed, he was through.

When clerks were short they often asked Mott to check their balance. That was a mark of respect they had for his ability. To a certain extent all the clerks in the place depended on him.

Mott didn't lord his ability over other clerks; soon enough some of them would be his superior. Ability didn't matter, not in the post office, payoff did, drag did, who you knew, that mattered. Anyone could advance.

It wasn't adding up. He wasn't going to balance, Mott knew it, he was sure of it.

He'd wanted a steady day tour and he'd paid off, once. That had been years back when he'd been on around the clock. Joining the local Democratic club, plus a small donation, got him an appointment with Mr. Hall, one of the assistant postmasters in Manhattan and when he got to Hall's office Hall ushered him in and said, Mr. Cooley said you'd be coming over, he spoke very highly of you. The tour sold for two hundred dollars.

He wasn't ashamed. You had to be a realist to get along in this world and if you wanted a day tour . . . Working all hours of the night had been a strain . . . But having to get involved with graft and corruption, petty as it was—it bothered him. It was dirty. He was confident that he could maintain his standard of living as a clerk; if he had to dirty his hands he would but he wasn't going to grovel in dirt for a promotion that wasn't necessary—so he stayed a clerk, he'd keep his hands clean.

"Balancing?" Long asked.

"It's off," Mott said, "the damn thing's off."

Some people explained Mott's ability by saying, He's an experienced clerk. The post office was Mott's life. Mott could let his eyes roam over the figures on a clerk's balance sheet and catch mistakes others would never spot. These mistakes were not of the simple addition or subtraction variety, the clerks themselves would catch those; rather, they had to do with digits that appeared to be what they weren't. Balance sheets were full of hastily scrawled easily misread numbers. Seven might seem one if it wasn't hooked firmly enough on top and two could be seven if there wasn't much of a bottom hook. With an extra curve to its bottom line two appeared as three and how many times was three taken for eight. That mistake was classic. Mott could see through the scribbling to the actual number. What an unusual field, he sometimes thought, to have talent in, post office clerking.

Now it all seemed useless.

When clerks hung up because Congress voted down a pay raise, when men stayed home because of a cold or bad weather, Mott would show. He'd never miss. Why, they'd ask. It made no sense. He knew that. He didn't dispute that. He said it was out of loyalty to the job and when clerks asked how he could have loyalty to this civil service job he couldn't give an adequate explanation. His fellow clerks resented him.

This was a bitter pill. He took pride in his ability, it was all he had. Yet, in the final analysis, what had it come to? Routes, rates, systems, zones: he knew all that. He did know it all.

Mott was sure the man standing in the back with his boss was an inspector and the inspector was there for him. Without confidence you're through, he was thinking. He watched them. I don't balance. He saw the boss point. The inspector seemed a man of preserved middle age and he held himself well. Mott felt a degree of relief watching him approach with his stomach muscles tensing to hold his belly in; he entered the cubicle. "Mr. Mott?"

"Yes."

"I've been talking with your foreman, Mr. Long."

Mott waited.

"Do you carry counterfeit insurance?" the inspector asked.

Mott hesitated a moment, surprised. "I used to but not any more."

"Why is that," the inspector asked, smiling—he was a big man, "do you think there are no more counterfeiters around?"

It was not widely known that clerks were responsible for the worthless money they took in. That was the system: each man was personally accountable.

"No. I know there are counterfeiters operating but I can spot a bad bill."

"Are you sure?"

"Sure enough to let my insurance lapse." Mott spoke not with confidence but from habit. He rubbed his fingers together nervously. His fingers were full of razor thin cuts; these cuts were black, dirt that had wormed its way under the skin. This was unavoidable, an occupational hazard: handling sharp new paper money caused it.

"You don't make mistakes, is that it?" the inspector asked, smiling.

Mott's eyes dropped to his yellow balance sheet, to the cut and dirty fingers that held it.

"Everything all right inspector?" Mr. Long called as he came close to the cage.

"Of course," the inspector said, "of course."

Long waved and smiled and walked on. That momentarily infuriated Mott—the wave, Long's cheery voice, Long's position, the way Long had avoided his eyes.

"Your boss," the inspector was saying, "tells me you aren't balancing out."

Mott nodded and stared down at the floor.

"Did you check your drawer to make sure no bills are stuck way in the back?"

"Yes."

"Did you check your sheets of stamps to see none of them are stuck together?"

"Yes."

"It's been humid lately."

"I know. I checked. Nothing's stuck together."

"Okay, I'll go over your balance one last time, after all we want to be sure. Every once in a while you hear about a body arriving at a morgue after it's been pronounced dead and then someone notices a heartbeat: let's be absolutely sure, okay Mott?"

If he'd let his stomach out he could be Santa Claus, Mott thought. The world was narrowing in. There seemed to be nothing outside, no 34th Street, no Macy's, no crowds rushing to Brooklyn, the Bronx, Queens.

"Figures don't lie, but I can't see where I went wrong," Mott said.

"Why don't you wait in the back till I'm through."

The inspector's eyebrows were almost colorless. Mott hadn't noticed that before. There was a wide mouth; his lips made a slit in his face. They were seated at a plain wooden table in back, neither had spoken.

"How did you know about my insurance?" Mott finally asked.

"We have ways of knowing."

There was silence.

"When I worked at the G.P.O. years ago there was spying over there. They actually had peepholes in the ceiling to spy on the clerks," Mott said.

"You're always being watched."

"Always?"

"Didn't you know that? What made you think you'd ever escape that, or that you should?"

"You mean there's the same thing here at Empire?"

"You want privacy, is that it? Like no one checking to see if you can balance out?"

Mott started to say something.

"Don't give me that. What makes you think you would have ever found out you don't balance if you hadn't thought we'd come? You did know we were coming, didn't you?"

"We, who's this we? I only see you."

"Okay, me. You know Mott, what religion calls evil I call guilt."

Mott hesitated. "I'm not religious," he finally said.

"Drop it," the inspector said, "do you play chess?"

"No I don't play chess."

"Me neither. My name's Mr. Z, perhaps you've heard of me? Sometimes people get my name confused and call me Mr. 2. 2 is easily confused with Z."

"I don't see how."

"There's room for confusion."

"They don't sound alike."

"Exactly," the inspector smiled. He spoke slowly. "That's the point."

"That's the point, I don't follow. What are you driving at?"

"Not me Mr. Mott, you. What are you driving at?"

With those words, spoken slowly and clearly, and with his steady gaze, it was as if the inspector had forced Mott to back away.

"A minute ago were you trying to say I feel guilty about something?"

The inspector shrugged.

"Were you?"

The inspector stayed silent.

"If you don't play chess why did you ask if I do?"

"I didn't mean to imply that I wanted to play a game. I'm sorry if my question confused you."

"It didn't confuse me," Mott said, "I—" He searched for a word. "—Can't you just talk straight and stop all this damn doubletalk."

"It's been my experience," the inspector said, "that whether or not a man plays chess tells you something about the man."

"What?"

"That depends on the man."

"Then where the hell's the chess come into it?"

"Don't get yourself worked up. Control yourself. If I'd known the question was going to upset you I never would have asked it. Look, I'm not saying it's a bad thing not to play chess. I don't play chess either."

"Oh, you don't play chess either. Because you don't I suppose it's okay that I don't. Who says I'm flattered to be compared to you? What an ego."

"Don't kid yourself, you're not like me."

Mott stared at the inspector. "This is unbelievable. I might have some guilt, who doesn't, but you, you're a goddam egomaniac you know that Z or Too or whatever it is you're called."

"That's it, good boy, here it comes. Come on, get it all out of your system," the inspector said.

A sudden look of surprise covered Mott's face.

A clamor from outside made its way in. It was a violent noise, a jackhammer drilling in the street, an emergency repair; it was dark out now.

Mott felt better now.

"Say," Mott said, "how's a guy become an inspector?"

"Oh," the inspector said, "it's just like anything else."

"Yeah," Mott answered, "I suppose. You know I used to work around the clock and it cost me two hundred bucks to get transferred to a steady day tour. Everything's either politics or payoff." He was thinking, I don't balance. I'm through. There was no more fear. "Do you agree with that?"

The inspector didn't answer. "I'm not here to tell you anything you don't already know, or anything you haven't always known for that matter. I don't have any surprises, there are no rabbits to pull out of the hat. Not everything's confusing. This is clear. It's all over. And you don't balance."

Mott nodded. The inspection was over. There had been mistakes. It didn't balance. There was no fear. He heard the jackhammer. The post office was deserted. The boss had locked up and slipped out, even the porter was gone. He was alone.

There was a leak in one of the underground pipes but it would all be taken care of; repairs were underway. Work would be carried on at night and the city could sleep; and the next day the post office would be open as usual; at most the lines would be unusually long.

The Inheritance Editor

THEY sat a seat apart on the park bench; there were cement supports under the bench which, in effect, divided space on top and created separate seats.

"Elaine, why won't you believe this, I'm in a race with the clock to save my life, my life, doesn't that mean anything to you?"

She sat stiffly. It was an odd sky.

"Next month, Elaine, I take the physical. I'm going to tell them you're pregnant, do you hear that? Do you want it to be a lie, is that what you respect in a man, the ability to lie?"

She shuddered slightly.

Several of the benches near the entrance to the park were filled with Negroes who looked with hostility at people as they entered. Teenagers, long haired, beaded, were in groups on the grass; they had guitars and transistors with them.

"If they want to induct me they'll have to give me a minimum of twenty-one days after the notice comes and before the induction. That gives us enough time, doesn't it? Will you please let me plant that seed? That will mean 3A. I'm looking for authority on various points but regardless of what

I find, regardless of what happens I'm not going, don't you understand that?"

White clouds were clearly etched against the steady blue sky.

"Jail, or exile, or staying here and dodging the law, is that what you propose for me? Isn't pregnancy preferable?"

There was no wind; it was summer, after supper, perfect, unreal, like a stage setting.

"I hate the President of the United States. Who is he now anyway? I feel as if he's personally trying to murder me. That might be psychotic, I don't deny it, but that's the state of my thinking at this point.

"I work seven hours a day. I work hard. You're no comfort, you're my wife, where's the sympathy, the understanding, why are you withholding that?"

"Stop it. Why do you do this to me," she said as her fingers twisted in the light sweater that lay in her lap.

"2A all through college, through law school, for what? Consider spending your time reading bills that have been proposed to the various state legislatures. Do I send this one to the Corporation Editor, the State Tax Editor, the Local Tax Editor, the Pensions Editor, the Stock Transfer Editor, the Incorporation Division Editor, the Wills Editor, the Labor Editor, the Social Security Editor? Do you think the hundred dollars a week I get is adequate compensation for that kind of drudgery?"

She stayed silent.

"Elaine, I want you to answer that. Answer that. Do you think the hundred dollars a week I get paid is adequate compensation for that kind of drudgery?"

Reluctantly, slowly she shook her head no.

Only a very few teenagers sat against the oaks and elms that grew forty and fifty feet from the path. At the base of the trunk of these trees, where the roots sank into the ground, no grass grew.

"Now, should I get paid more, which would you rather see, should I get an immense increase in salary or a more interesting position?"

"We're not a happy couple."

"Ah, good, you admit it, you admit that my life's hard, that it's drudgery. Now, you're my wife, you love me, why can't you—"

"Money isn't the problem. I won't discuss it."

"You have to discuss it."

"We have discussed it."

"I'm going to discuss this Elaine. Why must you be so unyielding?"

"Please stop," she said.

He went on: "How can I break through to you, what do I have to do?"

"Neither one of us wants children and I'm not going to let the army force us."

"Good, now we're getting somewhere, now we're dealing with the main subject. True, we don't want children, but my life depends on it, they're going to kill me so fuck our principles, survival's the basic principle, we have to be flexible, adjust, bend with prevailing conditions."

It happened imperceptibly: clouds were losing distinct definition, spilling slightly at their edges, tinging the blue sky with white.

"You're a con man," she said.

"Realities of life dictate my actions."

There were several water fountains in front of a squat brick building that housed the public toilets and the Park Department's maintenance and equipment rooms. All paths in the park converged at this central point.

"Elaine, I've had a change of heart, I want kids. I'm telling the truth, I want kids, take that button out of your twat and let's have kids."

A young boy approached the central area of the park; a bigger, older boy suddenly blocked his path. The young boy, trying to walk past him, was pushed and knocked down. He started up. "It's a free country, I can go anywhere I want," he yelled; the bigger boy laughed and shoved him back down.

Elaine looked back to her husband.

"Gary, we're not going to have children just for the army. Let General Hershey have children for the army. You don't want children, I know you don't. I'm not budging. You're just letting them bully you."

"No one's bullying me Elaine, I've simply had a change of heart, can't you accept that?"

A young Negro man who'd entered the park hesitated, checked, then walked past the benches with the Negroes, ignoring them, and directly toward the bench Elaine and Gary sat on.

"This is ridiculous," Elaine said.

The Negro's presence forced Gary to look up.

The Negro nodded. "How about some money for a drink?"

"I just gave away my last dime."

The Negro squinted down on him. "Dime. *Dime,* do you think I'd be standing here begging for a dime?"

Gary tried looking past him.

"It doesn't make sense," Elaine said, "it's ridiculous, I'm not going through this ever again."

"I never did this before, I'm a student," the Negro said. "I never begged." He was well dressed and his mustache was neatly trimmed. "I've got an Olds but no gas, I've got an eight hundred dollar check but it's still in the mail. That's not the point though, the point is that right now I'm broke and I want a drink."

Occasionally movie scenes were filmed here; although not a landmark, the park was famous for its offbeat population. The older Eastern Europeans, in whose neighborhood the park was located, avoided it.

Gary looked at Elaine. The man did not go away.

The older, bigger boy stepped out of the shadows when the young boy again appeared. He shoved the boy violently; there were cheers from the shadows; the younger boy fell backward, crying.

"Keep away, get the hell away from here," the older boy yelled.

"It's a free country," the younger boy screamed, "I'm going to tell mommy, I mean it."

"Ah, forget it," the Negro suddenly said. His belligerency vanished; he seemed a different person. "I was only kidding, it was only a game." He smiled, sat down. "It was only a game," he said. He was sitting in the space between Gary and his wife. "I wanted to see if I could beg." With his hands he made a motion that took in all the groups of white teenagers. "All these kids, freeloading, that's what they're doing, isn't it, that's the thing now, sponging, begging: I wanted to see if I could."

Gary, after a moment, seemed convinced. He moved over and made a bit more room. "They frequently bother me," he said, indicating the teenagers. "Everyone thinks you're rich if you sit in the park with a blue suit, white shirt and tie." The Negro nodded hello to Elaine. "I'm an editorial assistant in the Legal Documents Department of a publishing house. You think I'm going to give money away after that drudgery? Money's beans to me but that's not the point, I don't have an inexhaustible supply."

An old man, Negro, was lurching, stopping, steadying himself, moving all the while in the general direction of the bench.

"Change clothes," the Negro said, "that might help."

The old Negro was wearing loose khaki pants, badly beaten shoes and a Hawaiian sports shirt. His neck was especially thin.

"Mind if I sit down?" he asked.

"It's a free country," Elaine said. There was an empty seat next to her.

He was about to sit.

"I mind." It was the young Negro.

The old man straightened up and looked at him. His eyes were red. "You mind?" he said, astonished. "You shut up. These people said I could, who are you, what are you, I didn't ask you, you shut the hell up." He turned away and sat down.

A helicopter that shuttled travelers from the airport to the midtown heliport passed overhead. A harmonica joined the guitars.

"These days a college education's not an advantage, it's a necessity," the young Negro said.

The old man pulled a brown paper sack out of his back pocket. The young Negro muttered. The old Negro leaned forward and asked Gary, "Hey, you want a drink?" Gary shook his head no. Without taking the bottle from the sack, with only a bit of the neck showing, he drank; then he started to put it away.

"Give me a drink," the young Negro said.

The noise was gone from the sky. The sun had set and light was slowly fading.

The old man thought. "No, you can't have any." He put the sack in his pocket.

The young Negro leaned forward and looked across Elaine to the old man. "Give me a quarter."

This time there was no response from the old man.

"Hey!" the young man said.

The old Negro sighed, reached back, got the sack, handed it to Elaine, then slouched and closed his eyes trying for a comfortable position on the bench. The young Negro took the sack from her but kept his eyes on the old man. He was waiting. IIe kept staring. He was staring at the old Negro. He kept staring.

There was no moon. Clocks chimed the hour.

"Well, are you going to pass a glass?" the young Negro said.

The old man didn't respond. The cords in his neck jutted out.

Two men in green uniforms from the Park Department walked by picking up litter. A policeman was behind them.

"I can't take this without a glass."

The old Negro muttered.

"Oh Christ," the young Negro said, "don't tell me, is this wine?" He hesitated. "What is this, is this Silver Satin?" He tasted it. "Jesus Christ, Silver Satin, do you expect me to drink that? Wake up creep, this is the twentieth century."

A policeman walked by and two men from the Park Department followed him. There was trash around many of the benches.

He drank again, then said, "Here," and gave the bottle to Elaine.

"Who's he kidding? That guy drinks more Silver Satin than I do when I'm playing volleyball." The old man opened his eyes.

"Here," Elaine was saying.

The old man looked at the sack in her hand. "I don't want it."

She kept her hand out, as if he'd misunderstood. "Here."

"You keep it," the old man said.

She turned to the young man. He was thumbing through the *Pace College Student Handbook*. She held the sack out to him.

"I don't care for any, thanks," he said, barely glancing over at her, immediately returning to the student handbook.

She turned to the old Negro.

"I don't want it," he said.

Other clocks chimed the time.

"Well one of you better take it, I'm not getting stuck with this," she said. "This is ridiculous," she said, "I don't understand what's going on."

The policeman waited.

"Elaine, where did they go?" Gary repeated.

"I don't know."

"They were here just a second ago," Gary said.

The policeman looked at him.

"They were. It was an old bum's. I was just throwing it away for him. Look, I'm a lawyer, I work for Logan and Smith, Publishing—"

"It's against the law to have open bottles of alcohol in the park."

"What about all the panhandlers in the park, what about all the vagrants in the park, half those kids back there are probably smoking marijuana, what about—"

"Don't get hostile buddy."

"I'm not getting hostile."

"Don't get hostile with me."

"Okay, okay, I'm sorry."

"You were just doing an old wino a favor by throwing away his half-full bottle of wine for him."

Gary didn't say anything.

"Why'd you pick a trash can near the water fountains?"

"It was close."

"There are closer ones."

Gary turned to Elaine in frustration. "You mean they just disappeared, how could that be, I was only gone a second."

She shrugged. "They didn't just disappear, they just got up and walked away."

"I don't know if I should write out a summons or not," the policeman said. He seemed to be waiting. He asked, "Do you have any identification in your wallet?"

Taking out his wallet, Gary raised a five dollar bill so that it was obviously sticking out; then he handed the wallet across. The policeman took the wallet and when he gave it back the five was gone. "Okay mister, your identification seems valid, I'm not going to write out a summons," he said. "No summons this time. I don't know what your story is but don't let me catch you hanging around men's rooms and trash cans again, especially with open bottles of wine. You look a little like a pervert to me, the way you dress. Young kids have been bothered here, we don't need any more of your type. Try and clear your problem up, see a doctor if nothing else works. The park isn't a place to play games." He left.

Before sitting down Gary walked to the end of the bench and checked to see if the suitcase was still there, half hidden behind the bench; satisfied, he sat.

Elaine put the sweater on that she'd been holding.

"Do you think it's fair to place the whole burden on me?" Elaine asked.

"You're my wife," he said.

"That's right, but you're demanding too much of me."

"Don't you think it's right that the person who loves me should be the one who keeps me from being killed."

"Frankly Gary," she said, "that's laughable."

"Deferment's laughable? With your help I have a chance of being just about permanently deferred."

"Unfortunately," she said, "you won't accept what I have to give."

"Talk sense, you're the one who's against having a child, not me."

"You're a fraud Gary, you're a farce. This is cruel. I wonder if you have any real feelings for me. If you do then I don't see how you can ask me to do this. Don't say a word," she said, raising her voice as he was about to interrupt, "I'm not going to argue with you any more." Elaine pulled the sweater more tightly about herself. She studied her fingernails, then spoke coldly, clinically. "I don't think you're perverted Gary, I'll say that for you, we've had a good sex life."

"Just answer one thing, I want to know if you'll give me a son, Elaine, an heir, or if you refuse to."

"Let up Gary, leave off. I don't have your strength."

"When I tell the draft board you're pregnant and it turns out you're not, that's not going to reflect too favorably upon you, you realize that, don't you?"

"Stop it."

"It won't be interpreted as narrowly as you think," he persisted. "If I'm lying the lie will not only say things about me."

"I hate this. Why can't we ever say what we mean? It's all make believe, nothing's real, like that horrible suitcase you carry," Elaine said. "Why can't we try to be good to each other?" she said. She turned her face to him but he looked straight ahead.

It was chilly now. Hostile looking Negroes walked past the bench.

People on the grass were running.

Time passed. A clock struck.

There was a curfew.

"Are you just going to sit here all night?" Elaine asked.

"No," Gary said; he sat another second then got up, walked to the end of the bench, and took the suitcase. Slowly she got up.

He started walking down the path; he walked past young boys who were loitering in the shadows of the public toilets; they gestured suggestively. She walked beside him.

"I feel cheated," she said.

He didn't say anything.

The sky was almost all gray cloud. Not all the sky was made light that way; certain sections of the sky were clearly and deeply dark. It was an odd sky and, moonless, it gave an odd evening light.

A Matter of Survival

M EEK, indecisive, timid. That's what they said about Goodie Brown. He's harmless, he wouldn't hurt a fly, they said.

In his head Goodie Brown led an active life. His inner eye saw him do things that other eyes would never see him do.

Physically he wasn't imposing: short and dumpy, with a fringe of gray hair and melancholy eyes. Usually his pants were pulled around on his waist so that his fly was off center.

People were always stopping him from doing what he wanted to do, Goodie felt. They interfered. He kept a list of the people who had wronged him; and, like the other things that were important to him, it existed in his head.

The snow kept Goodie Brown home: a dingy two-room basement apartment with one street-level window. He made tea. On the sidewalk near the window was a battered garbage can. The kettle sang. Goodie didn't notice. It all seemed so futile. Tired. Forty-three years old and he'd had it. Again.

Goodie didn't see the blind man outside his window who was bending over to tie a shoe.

It wasn't hard for Goodie: He walked to the chest. Opened the drawer. Touched it. Took it. Raised it.

Goodie took the safety off.

"Hey," the blind man yelled, then came rushing down the stairs. Goodie Brown didn't hear. The blind man pounded on the door and yelled, "Open up, open up." Finally the sound penetrated and with a start Goodie realized someone was at the door. He stood where he was, called back from another world, blinking, groggy, unable to move, moving finally, putting the gun away, closing the drawer, opening the door.

The blind man spoke furiously, not trying to make sense, only sound: keep talking. Goodie didn't hear what the blind man said.

Goodie only heard the voices in his head: You're kidding— No! the first shot didn't kill him, he had to pull the trigger twice— Twice, Jesus, that takes— Goodie listened to the shocked, familiar voices, and he detected a note of respect.

The blind man, wearing dark glasses, was dressed very lightly, only a thin leather jacket, no hat, no gloves.

". . . and don't let financial worries interfere with your vacation plans, just call Household Lending," a transistor radio said, as a teenage girl walked past the apartment.

Young, the blind man had curly black hair and a clear complexion. Wind blew into the apartment. The blind man's shoulders took up the doorway; when he gathered his breath for a new burst of words, the depth of his chest was emphasized. He had a swimmer's slimness and fullness.

Like a man in a trance, Goodie looked at the magnificent physical specimen, who was standing in the bitter cold, speaking.

The kettle whistled.

The blind man held a black box which had printed on it: Sight Center. Talking rapidly, watching Goodie intently to make sure he made no sudden movement, the blind man opened the black box, and it was full of soap. Words: falling on top of each other, a torrent of them:

Scented—savory—sweet—three bars—two dollars—hand made—high quality—blind craftsmen—Sight Center—charity—business—sweet smell—

Goodie was freezing.

The blind man watched him like a hawk.

Two dollars. The kettle hissed. Two dollars. Snow was blowing in. Heat was escaping, the door was open. Go away.

How could he send this blind man away without a sale?

He wasn't going to buy the soap; he couldn't send the man away; faced with those certainties:

The gun. Raising the gun. Getting the gun, raising the gun. Raised. Pull—

"Well, how about one for a buck if you don't want three for two? A buck, a buck, c'mon, one lousy dollar," the magnificent physical specimen said.

The wind stung. Goodie started to turn to see if snow was accumulating in his apartment, and the soap salesman, spotting that sudden movement, the first sign of a door in the face, reached out: "Wait!"

They were having tea.

Pipes crisscrossed overhead: water pipes, steam pipes; exposed electrical wires dangled from the light fixture directly over the cramped kitchen table at which they sat.

"You don't have a dog," Goodie said.

"It's the dogcrap," the blind man answered, "I can't stand it."

"A cane? Can't you hurt yourself without a cane?"

"When I'm older I'll get a cane, when I'm a hundred."

Silence. The blind man seemed content. He sipped his tea and, finally done with it, spoke: "Yessir."

Goodie looked up; the blind man smiled. His white, even teeth stood strong and straight in his youthful face. "Yessir," the blind man said again, "if you make up your mind you can lick any problem." He paused for emphasis, leaned forward. "If you make up your mind to have faith, that is. Drive and willpower count, but they'll only get you so far. Faith, it takes you all the way."

Goodie looked over at the black box which the blind man had left near the door; it was wet and dirty, and the floor around it was turning muddy brown.

"I'm not blind," the blind man said.

"More dirt," Goodie sighed.

The blind man toyed with his sunglasses. "I'm not interested in conning you," he said, "that's why it's okay that you know I'm not blind."

"Much obliged."

"I had faith I'd save you."

"Suppose I didn't want to be saved?"

A cat stood on the grillwork outside the street-level window. It had cold, hungry eyes.

"This is my hustle," the blind man said, turning and pointing to the black box. "It's how I make a living: conning people. Getting them to buy my perfumed soapsuds. I used to be blind; that's how I got this idea. Then, one day, I got better; it was a miracle."

"A miracle?"

"An operation, okay, that make you feel better? You're

some kind of a cynic, aren't you? To me it was a miracle; how would you feel? One week I can't see, the next week I can. That's good enough for me to call a miracle."

"What's your name?" Goodie Brown asked.

"My life's full of miracles, like just seeing you getting ready to kill yourself."

"You shouldn't have interfered."

"Kurtz. How come you want to know?"

"I'm not going to buy your soap, Curtis."

"Why?"

"You're not blind."

"Can't afford it? A guy who was going to kill himself a minute ago, and now you're worrying about a buck?"

"You didn't do what you did just to make a sale, did you?"

"I got faith."

"That you'll make the sale?" Goodie asked.

"That when I leave you won't kill yourself."

"You shouldn't have interfered, Curtis."

"I'll make the sale, too. Why shouldn't I? I'm not harming anyone, I'm helping. I'm being honest. You don't lose a sale for saving a life."

"I don't want soap."

"Think positively."

"You're on my list, Curtis."

"What list?"

"My Christmas list."

The cat was emaciated. Its teeth touched the iron grill-work, and when its mouth opened, snowflakes landed on its tongue. The cat stared inside hungrily.

"I better get going," the blind man said.

"What about the sale?"

"I guess it'll happen now."

There was a loud noise—an eruption—and the drain in the sink backed up. Dirty water bubbled into the sink, then, a moment later, there was a sucking sound, the drain swallowed the water, and the dirt was left behind.

"That's your faith," Goodie said. "You make your faith do all the work. You just walk out, and if it happens it happens —but nothing just happens. You're putting all the responsibility on me. I shouldn't have to carry the burden of your faith." Goodie said that as he took the money out of his wallet.

The blind man was going to his soapbox, but he wasn't answering Goodie; he'd already had his say.

"All your stories have happy endings—" Goodie said. "A miracle gets you your sight back, you make your sales, you just save me in the nick of time. Everything works out for you."

The blind man handed over three bars of soap. "You won't harm yourself, will you?" He put his hand on the doorknob. "Remember, there's nothing so bad that you can't beat it."

Goodie rushed at the blind man, to grab him, to shake him, but stopped short, stunned: through the open doorway he saw a spastic walking on the sidewalk.

The spastic, a man about thirty, was being aided by an old woman; she looked like his mother. He had little control over his arms and legs, and less over his neck; yet over his lip was a pencil-line mustache. Goodie stared at that mustache.

The wind gusted and the snow continued to fall.

"Who gave you the right to interfere?" Goodie yelled.

The cat, shivering, starving, turned to the garbage can, sprang up, hovered a moment on the rim, then jumped down and in.

Realizing suddenly that he was alone in the apartment, Goodie turned from the door, ran for his gun, got it, then ran to the window and threw it open.

"See what I'm doing, look what I'm going to do," he screamed, sticking his head out the window.

The blind man was on the sidewalk.

Goodie took the gun and with his hand shaking raised it to his temple.

The old woman turned toward the shouting.

"You see, you see," Goodie screamed. "Don't you know that a man will do anything to live?" Through his mind flashed a picture of the spastic son, submitting on a chair: lathered up, head bobbing, heart pounding as the razor in his mother's hand came closer, closer— Goodie pulled the trigger once, twice, three times.

The old woman quickly pulled her son toward the corner.

This time there were no shocked, respectful voices in Goodie's head.

"Why did you have to butt in, why couldn't you leave me alone?" Goodie sobbed. He dropped the empty gun to the floor, the gun for which he had no—the gun for which he'd never had any—bullets.

The blind man stood at the open window. In a sudden frenzy, Goodie, who'd never before lifted a hand to anyone, lunged toward the blind man, leaped up, and struck him in the face. It caught him a glancing blow, knocking the dark glasses off his face.

There was dead white flesh where his eyes should have been.

The cat left the garbage can, pawed at the black box, which lay on the sidewalk collecting snow, then crossed the gutter.

Never Lose Your Cool

1953

I

H<small>E</small> turned an unfamiliar corner and heard footsteps quickly coming up on him. He started to run. He ran, people saw him run, they saw the two boys chasing him. The people did not try to stop the chase. William saw a vacant lot and started to cut through it, fell, was overtaken. When he got up they were standing right in front of him, two long haired, long sideburned boys, about his age, in their middle teens.

Although the two boys had been running hard, when they spoke it was as if they had not exerted themselves in the chase; they were not out of breath, they were not panting.

"Okay man, all I want is your wallet, hand it across."

"I don't have any bread."

"That ain't what I asked Jack. I just want to see your wallet."

"I don't have one."

"Sure Ace, but I'm going to take a look."

"Look man, why don't you just cool it and do like he says? There won't be trouble that way."

"That's right Ace, what do you want trouble for? You're just asking for trouble. What are you going to do with trouble when you get it?"

"Yeah, we want the wallet," explained the boy. "We don't want trouble. How come you want trouble?"

"Man, I can't understand these cats that go around looking for trouble."

"Well, I guess some cats just got eyes for trouble. I can't understand it either."

They talked slowly, clearly, so deliberately. As they took a step toward him he took two steps back. They came in slowly, seemingly carelessly yet actually carefully. They were positioning for the attack: craftsmen working at their craft, sharp, delicate, not one crude step, not one faulty movement. William kept backing up. He was about five feet from the wall when he pulled out his knife.

William did not carry the knife for protection and he didn't carry it for fun, although he used it for both; he carried it because he liked to put his hand inside his pocket and feel it.

The two boys stopped. They didn't turn and run when they saw the knife. William was frightened. They did not look at him any more. They ignored him almost completely. They paid no attention to the people on the street who could see everything. They spread out a little and while talking between themselves they forced him to back up, even more, even with his knife, even though they acted as if he were not there; back up, back up, more, ever so slowly.

"What do you think of a cat that pulls a blade?"

"I think he might be forcing someone to get cut."

"Yeah, that's what I think. Do you want to get cut?"

"Well, to tell you the truth, no, I don't think that I want to get cut."

"Man, I *know* I don't want to get cut."

"Yeah, that's right, I definitely don't want to get cut."

"Don't look like we'll get cut on then, does it?"

"No. I'll tell you something man, now that I've thought about it I'm damn glad that I'm not going to get cut because that can really be nasty, you know what I mean?"

"Man, I've seen some cats that look so ugly they hurt my eyes." He waited a moment then continued. "Do you know why?"

"Because they got cut on?"

"Right where people could see the scars."

"That's awful. But if there's a blade and if I'm not going to get cut, and you say you're not going to get cut, and it looks like someone might get cut, who do you figure is going to get cut on?"

"Well, it might be that cat that started all the action with the blade in the first place."

"That's just what I was thinking."

Slow, soft talk, purring, almost velvet talk, almost comical talk but talk that is electric and serious and adult. Walking in on William, spreading out on him, closing in a little, shuffling, positioning, forcing William back, all the way back now, still ignoring him.

"If the man had any smart he'd just drop the blade. He'd drop the blade and give us his bread."

"But if the man had any smart he never would have shown the blade, ain't that so?"

"Yeah, that's right."

"I guess the cat just don't have any smart."

Then one of the boys, with his head slightly down, lifted his eyes and looked at William. Directly. William could no longer move.

"C'mon my man, you made a couple of mistakes so far, you going to make another one now? Now what are you going to do?"

William could not keep his knees still; his nose started to

run, his eyes were watering and his cheek twitched. He wanted to urinate; a few drops escaped and slid down his leg.

"Look man, you're holding a blade, you don't want to do anything with it, why don't you just drop it?"

"Yeah, no one's going to help you. I'm not, he's not. You're going to have to help yourself because you're the only one on your side. Now, what are you going to do?"

William dropped his knife. As he did this the boy slapped him in the face, gently, playfully, like he'd pat a puppy. William felt a knee blast his stomach, then a thunderous blow on the back of his neck. He sagged down; not passed out. Not quite.

They kicked William. They took William's knife. They took the few pennies he had and then they sauntered off. He watched them walk away, unconcernedly; they walked with a certain air, an air that included pistol pockets and saddle stitching; he watched the people walking by on the street, the people who had witnessed this episode and who had walked right on by, the people who had averted their eyes after realizing what it was that they were seeing, the people who had been afraid to try and stop it, afraid to even call the police.

The two boys who had beaten him up were well trained, intuitively William grasped this, the people walking by were well trained, housebroken, William saw and accepted this. He was now determined that one day he too would be well trained, proficient, so proficient that he would have the power to turn strangers into sniveling and blind housebroken puppies.

William felt a profound admiration for those two boys. He desired their power.

The disdain they showed for everyone and everything;

the sneer attitude they carried like a sign on their bodies and faces; the attitude that said we can do what we want and when we want and how we want and if you don't think so why don't you step up here and try to stop us; they didn't respect anything, they didn't sweat anyone.

The way they walked; a slight bounce to every step, a litheness, a gliding more than walking. Not one clumsy movement. Surety . . . Cool.

II

William felt like punching someone, anyone. Blast, hard, in the mouth. There would be blood and spitting teeth; his hand would be cut and it would be painful. He wanted to feel a part of him hurt. William wanted to strike out. He felt the knot grow in his stomach.

He walked down the block to his car. Some of the people he passed were aware of him. William was starting to make it. He hadn't been tested yet; before the test comes you have to be worthy of a test. He had been proving that he was.

William got into his car. Not a hotrod with a packed hood and dual exhausts and an aerial that extended three feet over the roof of the car. Not a new black Fleetwood either. He was just starting to move up, he was ready to prove it.

Eighteen years old. William felt old, mature. Out of school for a year and a half, had a few hustles going, making good money, had a hard reputation, was respected. He learned his lessons well in high school and he had learned all that high school had to teach him by the time he was thrown out.

He parked the car in front of the school and smoked a cigarette. His hand did not shake as he smoked but he inhaled jerkily. He finished, locked the car door, and walked toward the gymnasium.

William was wearing a light blue topcoat with wide lapels. A belt was loosely strung around the outside of his coat and he had a thick loose knot tied in front of him. His pants were black, slightly pegged and sharply creased; his shoes had pointed toes and were gleaming black, polished to perfection. His hair was long and slicked back. William knew that he looked cool.

There was a basketball game scheduled today and William knew the gymnasium would be packed. William had seen many things happen at high school athletic events; he had participated in many of the happenings. He still retained a vivid picture of the football game he'd attended two years ago: the opposing school's side of the grandstand started to move, en masse, and like a wave they flowed from their side of the stands, through the end zone section, and toward his school's side of the stands. They met. Razor blades were shot from rubber bands. Brass knuckles appeared from back pockets. Lengths of lead pipe wrapped in tape connected with human shapes and caused dull thuds. The dull cracks of blackjacks. The screams of captured girls who were being toyed with under the grandstand. The game was forgotten, hysteria grabbed the crowd, the students surged forward, seeking the safety of the playing field. (This was a student body that was used to fights and flare-ups at athletic events, that expected and, by and large, looked forward to them, but the viciousness and savagery that were evident at that game were too much for most of them. They did not want to be involved, at all, this time.)

The feeling that William had (being a part of the small force that did not desert the stands) was a feeling that he could not forget. Standing there defiantly, not running, not moving, waiting, bouncing up and down confidently, trying to spot an enemy trooper within range, sensing that hundreds of people were watching him, or rather, watching all of the men who stayed in the stands, this was something he would never forget. This is what he thought about at night, in bed, alone, unable to sleep, when he wanted to think about the nicest thing that had ever happened to him.

On other occasions William had succeeded in partially recapturing that feeling, but never completely; either the audience was too small or the feat was not significant enough. He often imagined what it would be like if, instead of waiting for the enemy to advance, he were the aggressor, and if, instead of being a cog in the advancing machine, he were the whole machine. William spent many hours speculating on this unknown sensation, its rewards, the hazards presented by the difficulty of the task; he wondered, and he told himself that one day he would find out.

William was waiting, and after the wait was over, and after the feat was performed, he was going to tell the whole damn world, "Listen, I'm me and I'm the swinging cat. I'm cool, watch if you don't believe me, or ask someone who's seen me, he'll tell you, you'll find out. I'm cool, so my way is the cool way, don't try and mess up because remember what happened to the last cat who tried. I'm not a punk. I worked hard to get where I am and now I'm here baby so dig, I do what I want, you do what I want. What I say, me. I'm cool, remember that. Watch."

As he was on his way into the gymnasium he noticed a group of students standing in the hallway outside the gym entrance. He lit a cigarette, stopped to smoke it. The students saw him, and watched him, and their conversation slowly evaporated. The air thickened with the smoke from William's cigarette. William inhaled. One hand went into a big patch pocket on his topcoat. The other hung almost limply at his side. The cigarette hung between his lips. The smoke from the cigarette made his eyes squint. He snapped his thumb and middle finger together, rhythmically, as if keeping time to a rock tune. He nodded his head in time to the beat of his thumb and middle finger. He moved his left knee back and forth. The movement of his head, of his knee, of his whole body, was almost but not quite, imperceptible. He looked sensual, lazy, ready to uncoil, cool.

William walked through the crowd of students and opened the door to the gym. A boy sitting behind a desk at the entrance was collecting admissions.

"Half a rock pal."

William laughed; a low, calculated and controlled laugh.

"Sure." He made no move to pay. He stood right where he was, not looking at the boy, but letting his eyes rove through the crowd that was already seated.

The game was just starting. Not many people had their eyes on the entrance, most of them were watching the jump at mid-court, but those few who did happen to see William saw not only an ex-student but also a person who had not come to watch a basketball game. They sensed this and they prodded the person sitting next to them. Slowly the crowd's attention was transferred from the court to the entrance.

William was well known. To these high school people he stood for fear on one hand and freedom on the other. Freedom through defiance. The stands were full of people who nurtured the same dream he nurtured, but he was more advanced than they were. William felt the eyes on him.

"C'mon, it's a half a dollar."

William turned to face the boy. William's head bobbed slightly now. He opened his mouth wide, raised his eyebrows, sneered, and shook his head.

The boy did not know what to do. He wished that one of

the teachers would come over. He was sure that the teachers knew what was going on. He also knew that teachers never tried to break up fights in the locker room. The teachers had been teaching in this high school long enough to know when it is wisest to stay away, when it is time to keep the eyes straight ahead and unseeing. The teachers were hoping that William would just go and sit down. They didn't want his fifty cents. It wasn't worth it.

William was savoring every moment of the boy's indecision. He wanted the boy to ask him for the money, again. He wanted to hear that quivering voice, again. He felt powerful, knowing that the boy's voice did not ordinarily quiver. William knew that by now more people were watching him than were watching the game. He sensed the admiration, the adulation, the intense jealousy, the hatred. He gloried in it all. The boy's lips started to move. William wanted to expand his chest. He wanted to make his biceps bulge. Suddenly, tiring of the warm-up game, he walked away; a time-out had been called on the floor.

William walked out there. The cheerleaders who had run onto the court quickly headed back to the sideline. He headed for the referee. Tense inside, but loose and agile on the outside. He wished that he had a piece of gum to chew on. He felt that his walk was right. From the quiet of the crowd he knew that it was. The referee, out of a corner of his eye, could see William coming at him. He did not turn around to face William, to meet him head on, to look him in the eye, to try and stare him down, to intimidate him with age and righteousness. He did not want to. William reached him, tapped him on the shoulder, gently, two times. Very, very . . . lightly . . . politely. The referee stiffly turned. He seemed startled that it was William and not a fellow in a basketball uniform. The referee had known that William was going to force him to turn around; he had tried to hope that it was a player who was touching him.

No one moved. Anywhere. There were at least two hundred high school pupils. They sat, transfixed. Dreaming. Envious. The few instructors who were there sat shamed and afraid. William had everything in the palm of his hand. He knew it.

William pointed, almost daintily, at the whistle that hung around the referee's neck. He moved his finger back and forth, in pantomime, telling the referee and the crowd and the whole goddam world that he, William Baronofsky, wanted that silly goddam whistle that hung around that frightened goddam referee's neck. And everyone knew he wanted it. And everyone knew that he wanted it for nothing; and everyone knew that if he got it he could have everything.

William realized that if he made a mistake now he would have less than nothing. The referee did not know what to do. William waited, bouncing on the balls of his feet. Laughing inside a little, happy that the timekeeper would be messed up, happy that the ballplayers were not on the court even though the time-out was over. William wondered if this extra time-out could be considered an official's time-out. William laughed a little more. He felt giddy. William still bounced on the balls of his feet. Patient so far, making everything simple. Not a complicated plan; not a complicated objective; everything was simple. The referee looked toward the benches where the coaches sat. They looked the other way. The referee waited. William bounced and waited. The crowd sat, frozen. William deliberated. Should he try and yank the whistle off the referee's neck? If the string did not break and the whistle did not come off with the first yank the picture would not appear smooth and unmarred. That flaw could change everything. It could break the spell. He decided. His hand flashed to the whistle and pulled it and the string up over the referee's head. The whistle was off and in his hand. Free. Nothing had been touched; nothing was ruptured.

The referee stood, paralyzed. The crowd gasped silently, in awe. The crowd did not utter a sound but the pride, and also the revulsion, they felt could be heard quite clearly. That instant they all wanted to be William, regardless of how they had felt fifteen minutes before they walked into the gymnasium, regardless of the way they felt toward adults, regardless of the way they felt toward their parents and going to church on Sunday and helping old ladies with packages; any one of them would have traded places with William right then, gladly. They all ached to be William.

William tossed the whistle up and down a few times. He tossed it neatly and caught it neatly. Nothing sloppy, nothing that was not clear, hard, cold. He balanced the whistle in the palm of his hand. He looked at it. And smiled. He looked at one of the baskets at the end of the court. He looked at the whistle again. Long, hard. He smiled again. William started to walk, slowly, lightly, toward the basket, with his head still down, looking at the whistle, still balanced in the palm of his hand. When he was two feet from the basket he stopped. He threw the whistle, carefully, through the hoop. He caught it, glad that it had not touched the netting. After he caught it he looked at it again. Again he smiled; with his head down he almost started to laugh. He threw the whistle straight up and down a few times. He stopped doing this and thought about throwing it through the hoop again. He decided not to; it might touch the net and somehow spoil the picture. The picture he had created. He wondered what he should do now. The crowd was straining toward him, going with him, wanting him. Being him.

Turning, without thinking, without realizing what he was

doing, he hurled the whistle against the wall. There had been no warning. The crowd screamed. Loud. Everyone was caught off guard, unprepared. William included. The hypnotic spell had been pierced but not completely broken. The whistle had sliced the air like a saber. The sound the whistle made when it hit the wall was like the sound of a man dying, not afraid of death, but unable to keep from crying out.

William had not planned on any movement as violent as the one that had just taken place. It just happened. He heard the noise and he felt his cool leaving him. He started to feel lonely and afraid. Tired and empty. He felt untidy, almost undressed. Undressed and dirty. He almost panicked and ran. He wanted to let himself panic. He wanted to run, away. He bit his tongue to keep control. He realized the faster he ran now, the longer and farther he would have to crawl later. He forced his body to move. Slowly, disconnectedly, heavily. William plodded. He was stiff instead of loose. He made an effort to walk self-assuredly. He looked up at the crowd. He was surprised to see that they were still sitting still, staring at him, watching him with care, taking in every detail. He tried to regain his loose and agile walk. His body reacted jerkily, no longer a well-oiled machine; but it did do what he wanted it to do, more or less. He was surprised.

William could not unlock his car door. He could not get the key into the lock. He had captivated and then fooled those people, but he knew that he had lost. He realized he had failed. He did not know why. He didn't know if it was a lack of training or a lack of ability or perhaps even a lack of desire. He did not know. He realized he had almost won.

He wondered why he missed.

Portrait:
My American Man, Fall, 1966

Iᴛ should be Sunday. My American Man would be on the couch in the living room with his shoes off and feet up after a late breakfast of bacon and eggs and toast and coffee. The newspapers should be scattered. Everything's fine, a full stomach, and hours to look forward to, of peace. He's just seen Lindsay on TV. It's quite a thing when you stop and think about it, being mayor. A man in a position like that could really do something if he wanted, not that politicians ever wanted to really do anything except stay in office. That goes for all of them, they're all the same. Steal a dollar and you go to jail, steal a million and you go to Congress, that's the way it is, face it. Take Johnson. He made a speech in Toledo yesterday. Now they just got done with a race riot there, the Secret Service told Johnson not to go to Toledo, it was too dangerous there they said, so what's Johnson say in his speech when he gets to Toledo: that things have never been better. Politicians sure must think people are stupid. Over the noise of the kitchen faucet the phone was ringing. It would either be for Adele, her mother, or Jerry— What would you think of my growing a beard, Dad? Dye your hair, grow a beard, what do I have to say about anything— Don't politicians give the public credit for any intelligence? Adele's voice. This would be good for half an hour. Who the hell knew what this war was about? You're not for it, by the same token you're not against it because you don't like bucking your own government. I was down at Times Square when some of those peace kids were having a demonstration. Picketing, waving signs, not all kids, either. Terrible, terrible, this man next to me kept saying. They ought to take those people out, line them up against a wall and shoot them. You think the Commies would treat them any better? They love the Commies so much let's give them a taste of their own medicine. I have strong feelings on this subject but I'm pulled two ways. You don't want to be pushed around, but you don't want to blow up the world either, so you fight with one hand tied behind your back, it's crazy. I might only be a postal employee, basically I'm an uneducated person, but I'm not blind, I see the mess. It's everywhere. Just look at the niggers, they're rioting every week, who ever heard of this kind of stuff happening in America? There, that. Calling them that, I know it's wrong. Now either I shouldn't call them that or I should and I shouldn't feel bad about it, but neither's the case. Things were never better, things were never more screwed up, that's what Johnson should have said. Jerry's only twenty but he says some bright things. The kid has insights. Your whole thing, Dad, the kid says, is you believe in stereotypes when you talk about Negroes in general, but when you meet a Negro, one Negro, then you see him as a person, as an individual. That's one thing, Dad, you see Negroes as individuals. Well of course, what do you expect, what am I, Governor of Alabama, am I a southern sheriff? Haven't I known the colored all my life? Wasn't my boss for two years, Frank Philips, colored? Of course I see them as individuals. I just say one thing, they've got to help themselves, the government can't do it all for them. The Jet game would be coming on soon from Shea Stadium. Adele, how much longer you going to be on that phone? Why couldn't they stay in their own neighborhoods? They weren't like the Mets, this year they weren't clowns. Joe Namath. Four hundred grand. Who the hell knew how much money that was? With a bum knee. Four hundred grand. How could any man be worth that kind of money? They're taking the silver out of dimes because there's not much money around and they give this guy almost half a million bucks to throw a football. The Black Muslims, what was that nonsense he'd heard, their master plan: to have hundreds of thousands of babies, go on relief, drain the budget that way, and then use the money to buy some of the southern states and hand it all over to Castro's Cuba. Crazy foolishness, but these days you couldn't be sure. You ever see a politician die young, why should they? Post office clerks die young. The kid says the government tries to keep the war impersonal. For instance, dropping bombs; pilots don't see the people they kill: it's impersonal, and that's the way the government likes it. How about hand-to-hand combat, Jerry? Sure, Dad, if a guy takes a shot at you you're going to shoot back, that's not the point. Why do they blindfold a guy when he goes before a firing squad? To show mercy, so he won't see the bullets coming? No. If you want to show mercy you don't kill the guy. The blindfold's there so the guy who does the shooting won't have to look at the eyes of the guy who's being shot, the blindfold makes it easier on the executioner, it all stays impersonal. Maybe Jerry's right, I don't know. I remember the good old days when the bad guys were bad and you were glad you killed them. The Nazis, the Japs. Now you drop bombs and you hope you don't kill people, that's too deep for me. My mother-in-law's eighty-nine, it's time, what's she waiting for? Remember when the Giants and Dodgers were still in New York, those were the days, no complications. You

hated the Giants and loved Brooklyn. The Bums. Take
Branch Rickey, tightfisted, he didn't smoke, he didn't drink,
but he knew how to make a baseball team. Campy catching,
Hodges at first, Robinson second, Reese short and Billy Coxe
third. On Friday night you couldn't get a seat in Ebbets
Field if your life depended on it. Furillo in right, the Reading Rifle, he's a delicatessen man now, that's the last I heard.
Duke Snider center. The Duke of Flatbush. But they could
never get anyone for left. That's a truism of life I guess, nothing's perfect. Either you don't have a good left fielder or you
can't beat the Yanks, there's got to be something. Abrams,
Hermanski, Andy Pafko, Sandy Amoros, a whole slew of
them but they could never get that third outfielder. That
rotten so-and-so O'Malley: taking them out of Brooklyn,
anything for a buck, the almighty dollar. Robinson came up
in 1947, Dixie Walker was on the team then, the People's
Choice, he played right field like he owned it. But Dixie had
to go—so they traded him to Pittsburgh. Nothing's as simple
as it seems, the older I get the more convinced I become of
that, it's never all on the surface. We've all got our peculiari-
ties. Take me. For years I was a fanatic about cleaning my
fingernails. I don't know why. Then I started collecting the
dirt, saving it. I'd just been transferred from the floor over at
the G.P.O. to the stamp window. Naturally I started handling a lot of money and you'd be surprised how dirty money
is. I started hoarding that dirt. I got a coffee tin and kept it
in the bottom drawer of my desk at home and every night I'd
clean my fingernails and drop those tiny specks of dirt in
there. Pretty soon just collecting the day's accumulation
wasn't enough. I started carrying around an envelope and
two, three, four times a day I'd go to the john, clean my nails,
put the dirt in the envelope and then at night empty the dirt
from the envelope into the coffee tin. I came home one night

and there was Adele holding the can in her hand. She waited a minute, then said, What in God's name is this, I found it in the bottom drawer when I was cleaning out your desk, it stinks to high heaven. I didn't know what to say. Special soil to grow cucumbers in, I said, I've been saving it. I always could think on my feet. Then I started for the bathroom to wash up but before I got there Adele exploded, What kind of secrets are you keeping from me, you've got almost two pounds of filth hidden away in one of my Maxwell House coffee cans, why? Adele, I don't want to talk about it. What else could I say to her? I started for the bathroom again but she kept on yelling and screaming so I finally blurted out, Okay, you're right, I am keeping something from you. She got pale. Now you figure out what it is that I'm hiding, Adele, because I'm not going to tell you. As far as I'm concerned the matter's closed and I don't want to hear another word about it. Right after that I stopped collecting dirt. We never spoke about it again. Adele probably still wonders what it was all about. So do I. If Jerry would take my advice he'd become a politician, there's no better racket in the world. The post office is a pretty good job. Today especially, for a young man, I can't see anything the matter with it. You don't kill yourself, there's security, good vacation. Back during the Depression the post office clerk was king. Working steady, bringing home a salary every two weeks. Then, when a top clerk was drawing a big twenty-one hundred a year, Roosevelt gave a ten percent across-the-board cut. I never had any use for Roosevelt after that. The war broke out, people started getting rich . . . Four terms, the man was power crazy. It just went to show you how important a union could be, even one like the post office union, which by law isn't allowed to strike. If we'd had a union back in those days he'd never have gotten away with that cut. No two ways about it, today it's a damn good job for a young man, particularly if he knows the right politician and gets himself fixed up with a steady day tour. Not that it's any picnic serving the public all day long. Like the time I was working over at Empire and an old lady came in and asked for a Lincoln stamp. This was when first-class mail still was three cents so I gave her the Lincoln three and she shoved it right back at me and says she doesn't want that stamp, it isn't a good likeness. I've got a line out to the street, it's almost time to close the window, this is how you get ulcers. What do you mean it's not a good likeness? It's a poor replica, that's what I mean, young man, and don't be fresh. Isn't there a stamp where Mr. Lincoln's clean shaven? Lady— Watch your tone of voice with me, young man. Hey, Mr. Philips. I don't say another word, I just wait for the Assistant Superintendent to come over. What's the trouble, he asks. When she sees that he's colored the old lady says, My God, what's the country coming to, then turns around and walks out. The next customer says to me, You get people like that often? All day long, mister, all day long. I'll tell you one thing, there are better ways to spend your life than selling stamps, so what's Jerry want to do: quit school and join the army. Sure, great idea, go to Vietnam and get killed. With your beard. Why do you always twist around what I say, Dad. I don't want to join the army— I don't want to spend my life selling stamps either— I just want to get away from school for a while, I'd like to join the merchant marine, that's not joining the army, is it? Okay, fine, when the Vietcong's sending torpedoes at your ship you tell them you're not in the army, you tell them you're in the merchant marine and see how much it helps. If some of us had the same chances we give our kids . . . Well, what's the sense in thinking about that. I try to listen to classical music on WNYC sometimes, not to impress anyone, I only do it

when I'm alone, it's just for my own enjoyment. But it's no
go, after a couple of minutes my mind starts to wander, I'm
yawning, pretty soon I'm not even listening. Okay, you are
what you are, I am what I am: a slob: I admit it, I'm not
ashamed of it. There's this thing Jerry keeps raving about,
this poem, *The Waste Land*, it's so wonderful, so great, it
opened his eyes . . . I took a look at it and I couldn't make
heads or tails out of it. This is what they teach you in college? It's symbolic, he tells me. Symbolic, that's a new-
fangled word they're using in school these days. College
graduates, they can't add or spell, but symbolic stuff, that
they understand. What nonsense. You have dreams, Dad?
Yeah. Are there things in your dreams that don't make sense?
Yeah. Now do you think they don't make sense because they
don't have any meaning or because you don't understand
what they mean, in other words because they're symbolic.
That stopped me. He's some kid. What do you mean? You
know what I mean, he said. Imagine, a kid with a head like
that and he wants to quit school. What I wouldn't give to be
an educated man. You're an adult and you have to sit and
watch Westerns. Don't watch, they say. Sure, fine, I just
plunked down four hundred and fifty bucks for a new color
set and now I won't watch. They sure must think people are
stupid. Every day another ten, twenty American kids are
getting killed. They got Cuba and it's not hurting us, that's
the way I look at it. De Gaulle's crazy, maybe, I'm no expert,
I didn't go to college, but it looks to me like France isn't doing so bad with him. More money for taxes, everything's sky
high, you'll die before you get a doctor to come to your
house on the weekend: things were never better, Johnson
says. Our parents worked in sweatshops, they didn't know
the language, there wasn't any Relief—okay, you finally
show me that it's different with the colored, they were slaves,

this, that, they need special help, I'm finally convinced: the War on Poverty, Head Start, fine, good, I'm all for it—so now there's no money, there's a war in Vietnam. Maybe I'm stupid but it seems to me we got a war in Bedford-Stuyvesant. You take your life in your hands any time you go by there. Let's get that cleared up. The way I feel about it we didn't lose anything on the moon, what's the big rush, if we don't get there next year I won't feel I missed much, but I'll tell you what I do miss, I miss being able to walk down my block at night and feel safe. Broadway's a honky-tonk. There's not a park in the city that's safe, muggings, thuggings. Sure, big deal, the mayor goes for a walk through Central Park and no one rapes him so he gets on TV and says the parks are safe. Listen, if fifty cops followed me around I'd feel safe walking through the park too. Goddam politicians, how dumb do they think we are? I had a dream. I was in a room with college kids, it was some kind of party. I don't know what I was doing there. All the people were talking, they seemed relaxed and comfortable. Then I saw Jerry and even though he's twenty and I'm fifty-four, somehow, in the dream, when he came over to talk to me he was the father and I was the son. Why aren't I like all these other people, I asked him. He's holding a mixed drink and smoking a pipe. Why should you be, he says. The smoke was coming out of his pipe and it was getting hard for me to see his face. Because I want to fit in. Just be yourself. Be myself, what do you mean, aren't I myself? How do I know, Jerry says, I'm not you. I don't understand, what do you mean, speak so I can understand you. How can you understand me, Jerry says, you're still a child. He started to laugh at me. Then, a second before I woke up I heard what all the people were saying: Things have never been better, things have never been better, and they're all laughing. When I woke up

Portrait: My American Man, Fall, 1966

I was shaking, terrified. I can't get rid of that dream, I just can't get rid of it. Hey, Adele, give us a break will you, enough's enough. Listen, I better hang up, Harry's pestering me for something to eat.

An American Memory, 1966

I attend rallies, vigils, demonstrations. I am a man easily affected by ironies. Ironies purge me.

Not that I ever join in. I don't belong. This is a difficult time. People fast. Pray. March. I watch. I stand with the onlookers; sometimes the crowd draws close, turns ugly: taunts, shouts; wooden barriers are set up by the police; television reporters, film crews, cameras; the crowd grows red-faced, stands breath to breath with the pickets, fists shake. A night stick flies.

What can one do? One thinks of the Warren Report: But tell me Doctor, based on your medical experience would it be inconceivable, could you rule out absolutely the possibility, remote though it may seem, of a massive muscular contraction throwing the head back at the moment of impact? Is that out of the realm of possibility, Doctor? Well, no, nothing is absolutely impossible under those conditions . . . Thank you doctor. *Conclusion:* The President's head was thrown back by a giant muscular contraction which overcame the forward propulsion of the bullet.

The virtue of the Warren Commission finding is that it's somewhat existential: The individual can still work out his own destiny. I am curious. Ruby's cancer. Diagnosed as influenza. Jewish influenza. What can one do? Survive. Find an irony. Chew it. Suck it dry. Nourish yourself.

Peace marchers know me by sight. Questions. They ask me questions: Why are you always on the sideline, why aren't you here with us? Why don't you witness with us? Why? Questions. My father was a religious man; I was ten; he lost himself during the Holocaust. We kept him home, a thin brooding man with a hand like iron that struck out when small things displeased him. The war fed his deadness. The earth bled and I tried to please him. We spoke. "Ask," he would say, "What am I?"

"What am I?"

"You're a Jew.

"Ask: Why am I a Jew?"

"Why am I a Jew?"

"Because there are Germans.

"Ask: Why are there Germans?"

"Why are there Germans?"

"Because of God.

"Ask: Are we Jews really to believe, in the face of what is happening, that there is a God?"

"Are we Jews really to believe, in the face of what is happening, that there is a God?"

"Yes, we are to believe.

"Ask: How can we worship God?"

"How can we worship God?"

"The right question to ask because it does not relate to one's theology, it relate's to one's humanity. Repeat it."

"How can we worship God?"

"Because God exists does not mean he is to be worshipped. Because he is not to be worshipped does not mean he does not exist."

Personally I chose to marry a Gentile. We have a fine family: two boys, two girls. We're confident. We're going to adopt an American Indian and call him Morris.

Counter demonstrators appear at times, uniformed, disciplined, with swastikas on their arms, and they call the demonstrators unamerican. The banality of that irony forces me to spit it out; There is no nourishment there. I see that not as irony but as, for a rare change, the real world impinging on reality.

Last summer there was a documentary on educational television about the Warsaw Ghetto. There were diaries, artists' interpretations, captured German film. Film makers are everywhere. A violin cried in the background and I danced. My wife wouldn't watch. I cried. I felt fine, purged.

Adenauer visits Israel. The Holy Land. The Jewish State. He is old and bent and withered and they riot against him; they riot though Germany sends them arms. The rioting is condemned and those who condemn the rioting say: The Jews ought to forgive. They do not mean that. Adenauer does not want the Jews to forgive; he and the world care nothing for the Jews forgiveness; he and the world want the Jews to forget.

But my memory shines. It lights the way. It clears the path. I remember paternal madness. Cold soup made my father lose his temper and he would slap me in the face; genocide made him lose his mind and the only answers he could accept to his questions were the answers he put in my mouth. I recognize paternal madness. The Fatherland. Support our boys in Vietnam. Support our boys in Vietnam. The Fatherland. Paternal madness. Memory. It lights the way.

In Equal Parts

His wife had been gone two weeks. The house was a mess. He cooked for himself. Dust accumulated. What was he going to do with the summer? The sink filled. It was depressing coming home to an empty house.

He didn't want to take a chance on spoiling it by making a move. When had the woman come in? It was Sunday. She was beautiful and her eyes were on him. Only an hour or so ago he'd returned from a weekend with his wife.

She was on vacation in the mountains with the children for the summer, staying at a bungalow colony that offered many features of a resort hotel. He'd thought this would be a dream come true, being alone for the summer.

How could he have been so stupid? Why had he gotten into this? A month in the mountains would be fine, his wife had said. Like a glutton he'd insisted she go for the full season, the whole ten weeks. They could finally afford it, he'd said, and he'd make occasional runs up from the city. Much as the impulse was there to cut loose, prowl, run around, now that he had the chance he couldn't. He should have known in advance it would be that way, that it would be impossible for him. He was full of ridicule for himself; what had he thought would happen, had he expected that something would simply be dumped in his lap?

A few minutes ago he'd looked up from his drink and there she was. She'd simply appeared, materialized.

It had nothing to do with ideals or morals; rather, it was his makeup that wouldn't allow it, his sense of dignity. He was embarrassed by himself in equal parts by what he might do and by the restraint that kept him from doing it.

Something was lacking. The lack that he felt was not in his marriage but in his life. He knew that was an odd distinction to make, yet he believed it was valid. He tended, occasionally, to be moody and jumpy around his wife but it wasn't because of her, he had no complaints about her. This was something very private.

And it wasn't unique. Many of his old high school friends who, like him, were married and in their mid-thirties, shared this feeling, this discontent. Yet they seemed strangely different from him. They acted in ways he found unappealing: going to a prostitute, that was so calculating, so callous, it somehow completely missed what he was after. Having your own bookie and your own madam: that satisfied them and gave them what they felt they were missing, their sense of adventure, of life.

He was now at the Crystal Ball, a supper club on Utica Avenue in the East Flatbush section of Brooklyn that tried to cater to a certain class of clientele. There was carpeting, a hat-check girl and dim lighting; bar whiskey cost a dollar and Canadian Club a dollar twenty-five. There was no beer. The bartenders wore red vests and black ties. There were several tables, each had a thick red candle with white drippings. The only items on the menu—there was a small kitchen in the rear—were shrimp cocktail and steak. A middle-aged crowd, by and large, patronized the Crystal Ball, it didn't attract a young set; and at night, no matter how noisy it got, there was never any roughhouse.

He'd been raised and still lived in East Flatbush. Generally speaking his friends had either not started or not finished college; they'd gone to work in their father's or a relative's store or business and by now they were earning respectable incomes that they spent; they enjoyed the trotters, Miami Beach and Grossinger's. He wasn't as flashy as they were, he thought. Sometimes he thought he wasn't as honest and open. Maybe it was inhibition that was keeping him from what he wanted.

A bachelor party had been thrown for the last of his single friends two years ago. A suite of rooms was rented in a midtown hotel and it was arranged for two girls to put on a show. Halfway into the program one of his friends, Artie— Artie was thirty-four years old at the time with three children, the oldest thirteen—made a lunge, grabbed a girl, and then, in front of them all, got his clothes off and climbed on top. There was whooping and drinking; the girls finally managed to hustle themselves into the large double bedroom. The guys were all going in; there were fourteen of them at the party. Only he and another man—the man was in his late fifties or early sixties—hung back. This older man worked with the groom at the groom's father's furniture store. Artie, taking it upon himself to see that things ran smoothly, was motioning the man into the bedroom. "Go ahead," Artie said, "go ahead in, it's free, it's all taken care of."

"No," the man said, waving him off, "no, you go ahead and enjoy yourself, don't worry about me."

Artie shrugged and turned away. Then he said, "Say, Stan, you haven't gone either, what's the matter?"

He didn't know what to say, he felt awkward. "I'm not in the mood."

Artie stared at him, it quieted in the room. Then it passed;

that was all. But for a moment it had been tense. There had been more to it than met the eye and not long after that evening he came up with the idea of a summer alone.

This age, his age—thirty-five—was in the middle, neither here nor there. He was starting to look old but he felt young. While later on he might look back and find it a good time— he had his health and he was starting to prosper—that would be a distortion of memory. It was a question of attitude: he was fighting settling down, and a kind of turmoil ensued. He should have been satisfied. By almost any standard, by his own admission, things were going well. He couldn't put his finger on it. He still had dreams, hopes. As he said to himself, there were things—undefined—that he yearned for. At times, when the yearning was acute, he was difficult to live with, irritable and short tempered. Seeing how he'd acted, he'd sometimes grow disgusted and accuse himself of being childish and immature. The sense of dissatisfaction with his life that sometimes gnawed at him was nothing more than nervous energy, that's the way he'd mock himself; he just needed to find some wholesome outlet for this excessive amount of nervous energy that he carried around—maybe he'd try handball.

He'd hoped that this summer, with his wife and children gone . . . Nothing worked. It hadn't turned out; if anything, it had backfired.

On Friday morning, out of loneliness and frustration with himself, on the spur of the moment, instead of going to work he'd driven to the mountains.

"My God," his wife said when he tapped her as she sat in a beach chair by the side of the pool, "what are you doing here? I thought you said you'd probably have to work this weekend. Why didn't you let me know you were coming?

You could have written or phoned, there are phones you know."

"I thought I'd surprise you."

She stood and took her sunglasses off. "You look thin, aren't you eating?"

She had him by the arm. They were walking. She was very close, clutching him.

"Where are the kids?" he asked.

"Taken care of at the daycamp until it's time to eat, don't worry."

She locked the bungalow door behind them.

It had been a fine weekend. Had he stayed in Brooklyn he might have cracked; why should he subject himself to that torture, it was madness. He played with the children, sunbathed, relaxed. The inner turmoil was gone and it seemed to him that he had everything he wanted. Driving back to the city on Sunday he was in high spirits. Home it soon ended. Who was he kidding? He wasn't home half an hour before he began eating away at himself: his chance, his golden opportunity, this summer, what would he do now, spend the rest of the summer running up to and back from the mountains? Wonderful. What a hero. He tried watching television, couldn't, showered, put on fresh clothes and drove to the Crystal Ball.

There were twenty-three stools running the length of the bar and he sat on one at the midway point. The bar itself formed a right angle as it hooked to the wall and because the woman was on one of the stools at that part of the bar they could look at each other almost full in the face. She was in a party of six, three couples.

What was going on? She would turn and talk to the woman next to her, but even while doing that her eyes would drift back to him every few moments. Was she flirting, trying to pick him up?

No.

If he could only be like his friends, gaudy, or at least less self-conscious—they didn't agonize the way he did, he knew that. But he wasn't cut out for their style of life. And what a madam had to offer was not what he longed for.

This was no prostitute, no cheap barroom hag. She wasn't trying to pick him up but she was coming on.

She was drinking something on the rocks; the ice glittered. Her face was flawless, perfectly oval. About twenty-seven or twenty-eight years old, she had soft honey-blond hair that she wore swept up and with her off-the-shoulder dress there was one long sweep of skin from her firm and round arms and shoulders to her long, elegant neck. She sat very straight on the stool; she had full breasts; she was beautiful.

The woman smiled slightly at him now, looked for a long moment, then lowered her lids: not to put him off, to lead him on. There was no pretense.

The bartender caught him staring and winked; he glared back, ordered, pushed a bill toward the bartender, and put his eyes back on the woman. Behind the women who were seated on the stools, stood the men, holding drinks, laughing, talking.

It continued between them while they went through the motions of normalcy: The woman spoke at times to the people she was with; he carried on bits of mechanical conversation with the bartender, he moved his stool so two men could stand together, he passed an ashtray . . .

He knew it would end everything if he tried to make a move, if he approached her. He was flattered that she was interested in him, that she'd picked him. What was happening, what was it all about? This was not just a sexual attraction, it was more: a giving, a getting; it was almost spiritual between them: the openness, yet a mystery, the intense feeling . . .

The man the woman was with, after weaving slightly on his way to the men's room, was now paying attention to the other women, putting his arm around their shoulders, peeking down a dress front.

There were things, not yet clearly formulated in his mind, that he wanted to tell this woman, but none of the clichés. While he was bending over picking up a gold lamé purse that the lady next to him had dropped on the carpet, it happened: without warning, without a last look: the six people started to leave. The men had backed away from the stools, it was ending; he looked up, he didn't know what to do.

They came around in a group and started walking the length of the bar to the door. The man now had his arm possessively around the woman; with great care he guided her. She turned away and avoided his eyes; she waddled past him gracelessly, very pregnant.

He was shocked, numbed.

The door opened and the party was gone.

The way a fighter in trouble tries to clinch, then ride out the round on instinct, he tried to let only his body operate. He turned back to the bar, found his drink—spiritual—finished it, collected his change—openness—put a bill under the glass for a tip, took a toothpick from a shotglass, then started to leave but sat back for a moment: what a con job. A spiritual relationship.

He was numb. He wondered if anyone had ever been had so completely.

He tried to tell himself to stop being foolish, the woman

probably felt ugly and wanted some attention, she'd made big eyes at him and he'd fallen for it, so what? That's all there was to it, what else had there been to it?

He went home; he felt old in an odd way, tired. And he thought of the old joke—wasn't it about Jack Benny—that he was thirty-nine going on seventy. That was the way he felt.

His wife returned at the end of August and saw the change in him. He was no longer restless. He was a different person —in subtle ways, ways only a wife would recognize—and his manner seemed to her so totally free of edginess that she couldn't get rid of the nagging doubt that he was having a terrifically happy love affair.

The Story of a Story

WHEN the conclusion of a certain kind of story is so powerful that it will blot out all else, to tone that down, to keep the concluson from overshadowing the full body of the story, any one of several possible devices may be employed. A successful technique the writer of serious fiction sometimes uses when faced with this is foreshadowing. In Faulkner's "A Rose For Emily," Emily holds onto her lover's body for years; this is discovered at the end. To in part counteract the sensational aspect of that revelation, we learn early in the story that, out of anguish and grief, she, on the death of her father, refused for several days to give his body up for burial. Somehow that helped prepare the reader for the shock at the end. When faced not only with a powerful ending but with a plot so engrossing it will call undue attention to itself if not somehow tempered, the author may simply begin with plot summary. In Hawthorne's "Wakefield," where a man walks out of his house and away from his wife for twenty years, lives in the house around the corner and then, for no apparent reason, returns, we get all this in a single paragraph. After that Hawthorne goes ahead and replays that one paragraph, now taking many pages to fill in the story.

With my story it's not necessarily the impact of the conclusion or the magnetic quality of the plot but, if you will, the patness of it all that makes me wary. It may seem overly contrived, too blatantly manipulated, all the strings are tied together at the end: It may not be fictionally believable. I'm ruler, king, creator, god, in short Paul Friedman, author. I could change the end and that would eliminate the need to go into all this, but I reject that. There are a variety of reasons for my doing so, some of which will shortly out; for now let's simply say I choose to experiment.

No changing. No summarizing (summary blunts interest in the plot). No foreshadowing (foreshadowing dulls the impact of the conclusion). Authors, when they give up, for instance, impact, hope to gain more than they give. I've warned this ties up neatly; that costs me something. By reminding you this is fiction, not fact, I'm giving up the illusion of reality; authors work to achieve just that. A widely held tenet in the world of reality is once something exists or happens, it, therefore, automatically exists or has happened. Mere occurrence is proof conclusive; degree of improbability, matters of implausibility immediately become immaterial. The inconceivable unquestionably is if it turns out to be. It's only in the fictional world—the world I live in—that the illusion of reality must be achieved. Clearly this totally unrealistic criterion we've developed for fiction places an intolerable burden on certain kinds of stories.

I'm giving up the reality of illusion. That costs. That's expensive.

Inevitability. (Pat ending.)
There is the fine kind where the reader after finishing the story says yes, of course, that's the only way it could have

ended. Somehow, after the fact, there's the realization of the fact's inevitability.

There is, of course, another kind, finer I think. Terrifying: because you know what is going to happen, you see it coming, you sense it can't be stopped, it can't be prevented even though tragedy will occur. You sit on the sidelines watching, waiting, knowing, helpless.

The King killing.

The shock of King's death. Shocked? Why? Surprised? Why? Didn't we know it was likely he'd be killed? We knew. And the shock came from that: that we knew, and, knowing, still we couldn't stop it, still we didn't prevent it.

How feeble, how weak, how puny. The shock deals with that, our own fallibility, our own mortality: Each time we face that truth it's a fresh jolt:

Pat.

I'm author. In control. I guide. Geometric correctness. King's death had that: inevitability. Form is one thing but for an author to be a character he has to be content. That's part of the experiment. I'm wary of fictional geometric correctness: What's factually permissible may be fictionally fraudulent: too neat.

Nevertheless, can't you see the fallacy of changing this end; I want to try this; what an opportunity, I'm the author, Paul Friedman, I've never been contented and I'm trying. Inevitably.

I'm a thinker, not a doer.

Exploring interests me, I'm an explorer.

Natural phenomena interest me.

My height interests me. So do my eyes. What do I see? How high am I, I'm curious. I've been asking for years and the only answer I ever get is, Five feet so and so. Crap. Rulers are notoriously inexact.

Measuring sticks are machine made, mass produced, yet you always get an answer to the inch.

If I'm king, nevertheless I grant my kingdom's insubstantial, don't think I have a big head.

What else? My age? You see my predilections, my inclinations.

My thoughts generally aren't startling. How could they be, why should they be? If you're a doer you do, if you're a thinker you think, period. You can cope with the idea of a mediocre mechanic, a dumb doer, why be surprised by a thoughtless thinker? We're surrounded.

I'm a thinker of a kind, a writer: I operate on approximately the level of daydream.

If one were to write about a doer, plot would revolve around doings: joining the army, fighting a battle, going to town, getting drunk . . . Writing about a thinker, the plot's made of his mind: with its ins outs ups downs curves edges ledges. A thinker: We pick him up approaching new territory. There's some tension: Will he try it, will he plunge in or won't he? If so, will he follow in hot pursuit regardless of where it leads, or will he grant sanctuary beyond some certain parallel of discretion or river of interest?

In. Having plunged, one wonders: Will he crack, snap, flip, come out starved, vacant eyed, mute? Or will he emerge smiling, the conqueror, his photo taken as he stands triumphantly with one foot upon the dead carcass of some lionized concept, looking English, will he have his foot on an elephantine notion—in short, some bull?

Many layered: all within.

Mind. Body. 1) Mind. 2) Body. Sometimes in harmony, sometimes warring.

Rendered impotent. Impotence. There's no denying it, the eyes of truth stare you in the face.

The mind, the mind:

To the desk, nine in the morning: Start thinking. Stop. Get up, go out, buy a paper. Takes an hour. Ten, coffee. Ten thirty, a letter. Eleven, tempted to lie down for some minutes, only a few, sleepiness, fatigue, eyes heavy, a whole day ahead, mind's blurred, not sharp, can't think. Twelve. Hungry. Eat. One: the news, threat of war, buy a paper and pretend you're seeing what the columnists say. So on through the day. Late at night fatigue gone, sleepiness of the day gone, now last chance, it's a new day, I haven't worked, last chance to sleep: if I want to, it's that simple, if I want to avoid tossing turning twisting, if I want to sleep I have to work. Alert. Door locked. Could, could trick self. Could postpone the trip in, that exploration.

How? Exercise. Do exercises. Mind and body, warring. Partners. Lift weights. Tire body, wear off tension, release energy. Exhaust body. Then sleep. It works, I know. I know. Or, better, work: a while. One idea, one sentence, then, euphoric, jump up grab barbells dumbbells lift pull strain pant sweat grunt more weight pull stretch sleep.

It works.

It works.

It works.

Multi-level divisive warfare. Many layered. Us.

This whole notion of intercourse that's been going around for the last decade has done more than anything I know to ruin the pleasures of masturbation.

Or cards.

Here you don't tire the body but dull the mind. Solitaire. Game after game, over and over, endlessly. Eight games, ten games, twenty. Shuffling's a problem. Overcome it, outsmart it, use your head: don't shuffle, collect cards and deal out poker hands, that gets them mixed.

Tricks.

A guess: Sartre would knock forty points off the top of his IQ for four inches of additional height. That's not original, Mailer probably first made the observation. Sartre should have lifted. It's an immense cellular truth: stature counts, stature matters; heights, like realities, exist.

For years I mailed my stories out, they went about, I worried constantly they'd be returned rejected. They were. Mental health's important. One keeps one's body sound, the mind's entitled to the same treatment. I began sending out five originals of the same story: Multiple submission is forbidden. It did wonders, tricks and games. I had to hope my story would not be accepted at two magazines at the same time, I worried constantly it would be. My hopes were constantly fulfilled, my worries never justified.

Writer. Mental health. Mind. Preserved.

Originally I was going to call this, The Autobiography of My Wife. Then I came up with the current title:

The Story of a Story

It's January 2, at the airport.

"Will you love me when I'm back in New York?"

"I'll love you even when you're dead, Grandpa," Karen said.

There was a startled silence.

Now he is dead.

Karen cried, sensing from the silence that she'd said something wrong.

He raised me but he was not my father.

On the third floor of a high school in the classroom. The door is locked, two boys are holding a third boy by the ankles out the window. He is dangling head first. The bell has not yet rung. The teacher is now trying to get into the classroom but the door is locked and no one's opening up. There's a crowd of students below; they're waiting.

Later, after the boy has been hauled in, after the teacher had been let in, after the class, the boy was asked how he felt toward Lenny now. Lenny had been one of the two boys holding him by the ankles. It had been Lenny's idea.

"You must hate Lenny."

"Man, you kidding, you crazy? When he pulled me in the only thing I felt for him was love for not dropping me."

The teacher, who taught little, learned much and left thinking he knew nothing.

My neighbors: women who used to give Tupperware parties, men who bowl on Tuesday and Thursday nights in league . . . Not quite, but there's truth in that description. Times change. My neighbors invited a John Bircher, just to hear what he had to say, to hear both sides. I talked with him afterwards. He frightened me; I lift weights for strength, he talks to God. Martin Lucifer King, Communist devil, that sort of thing.

The old chestnut: Eisenhower is for integration, but gradually; Stevenson is for integration, but moderately. It should be possible to compromise between those two extremes: My neighbors.

Once two magazines took the same story. I let it go, I changed the title. I list both when I send out lists. So far so good, no one's noticed.

Whatever made you ask that?
Just something I was thinking about.
You were thinking about that?
Yes.
How come?
I don't know, it just came into my mind.
Come on, get off it, do you expect me to believe that?

Why shouldn't you, it's the truth.
In a pig's eye.
What do you mean?
You wouldn't know the truth if it hit you in the face.
I can't believe this, what's this all about anyway?
Figure it out yourself.

You're a spy, that's what you are, it's the only thing to call
you. She was starting in again. Sh, he snapped. Then he said,
I remember the first time I went to the toilet with my mouth
full of food. I wondered what would happen, I was a kid,
six or seven, I wondered what would happen with things
going into me and coming out of me at the same time. Give
me a piece of paper, I better write that down. That filth,
you want to write that down? Yes. You really wondered that,
what sort of filthy mind do you have anyway? Actually it
just now popped into my head but maybe I'll be able to use
it sometime. How disgusting. You're such a calculating person, but I wish you'd had the good manners to do that, to
make things up instead of spying and putting down exactly
what happened.

Stop bullshitting, the only thing you ever made love to
was your fist.

Christmas decorations are out, the season of good cheer.
I passed a little boy coming home, snot nosed, maybe seven.
Teeth chattering, lips chapped. Skinny. Wearing levis and
wet shoes; a thin jacket. The soft pink flesh of the inner part
of his lower lip was divided from the flaking chapped outer
part by a thin line of grime. He was throwing snowballs and

his fingers were wet and red. He didn't know how cold he was, how blue. A bus was coming, he watched it come, waited, threw two snowballs, hit it twice. Yippee! he yelled. His last snowball, before I turned off, hit the bullseye: the middle of a red STOP sign on the corner. He noticed me. Hey mister did you see that? I nodded yes. I'm going to be a pitcher, he said.

He had no idea how frozen he was, or even that he was.

My neighbors, they too are suffering.

I'm a writer, they think I'm interesting.

I finally got that bastard where I want him, by the balls, and now I'm going to squeeze.

Two hills of earth stood a few feet from the shanty—a trailer on blocks. Jerry held the hose low so the old man could pass. The old man stopped, there was something in his hand.

Mr. Steel was the renting agent. Ray Loundes was the super on this ten-million-dollar job, a seven-story luxury apartment house. Tons of dirt had been hauled over by Pacelli Landscaping. Laborers thinned it by removing weeds with rakes and pitchforks. Then the soil was shovelled into wheelbarrows and pushed to where the shrubbery would be.

Jerry, washing the sidewalk down with the hose, looked at the old man.

They'd been doing it day in and day out for weeks; it was amazing. She was going away for the weekend.

What am I going to do, he said. There was a suggestive leer on his face.

What do you mean?
You know what I mean.
Satisfy yourself.
Sure, great idea, how?
She picked up her luggage.
Jerk off.

Did you let one?
What?
Did you let one?
They'd finished making love.
You always do that.
I have a sour stomach, what do you want from me?
God what a rotten smell.
I get fierce pains if I hold it in, you know that, what do you want from me?
Silence.
Did you let it on me?
No answer.
You did. You let it before you turned around, you weren't turned the other way. What's happening to us? Oh Jesus, what's happened to us?

He gets there late and stands in the huge crowd of jeerers. He sees a sign a high school boy next to him is holding. He sees a big red STOP sign drawn at the top of the boy's sign. He sees only STOP THE WAR, but below WAR it says DEMONSTRATORS. He doesn't see that bottom word. Cursing, he grabs for the sign, saying, What do you mean stop the war? He gets the sign, rips it in half and throws it to the ground. The boy is stunned. (My sign, my sign.) Legionnaires yell, What are you doing he's on our side. He hears, but he seems unable to comprehend. Then he picks up the two pieces of the sign and holds them together. He says, Oh shit, oh shit I didn't know. He says to the boy, I'm for the war, I'm for the war too, I'm sorry, I'm for the war.

Then someone raises a sign saying, King For President.

"Say, what's it cost a man to have a job like this done?" the old man asked Jerry.

"Oh," Jerry said, then the cement mixer started up and he didn't have to answer.

The old man waited. "How much, about a thousand dollars?"

Jerry washed down the sidewalk. Seeing the old man approach, he'd played the stream of water up the driveway he and his partner had just finished cementing. It had been difficult getting the pitch just right. That was particularly important in the back yard; if the pitch was right the water would roll to the drain and there would be no puddles after a rain. Puddles eroded cement. If water collected ice formed.

"We give out estimates for each job individually, no two jobs are alike. You got a job you want me to take a look at, or you just wonder about prices?"

"Oh, I don't wonder about prices at all. I'd give you a job, I need a new porch put in, I'd give you the job if I thought I'd live long enough to see it done." He waved his hand and there was an envelope in it. "I write my son once a week. You think he cares? I can't get excited." He pointed. "Bum ticker. The doctor told me not to get excited." He looked at the envelope. "I ought to go mail this." He lit another cigarette. "You think he cares if he hears from me or not?"

"Don't you think you ought to take it easy?" Jerry said. "You're getting yourself pretty excited."

"Upset?" He laughed. "You show more interest in me than he does. Christmas is the only time I get to see him and that's if I fly out there." Suddenly he tore the letter up. "How can you help getting excited? Some gratitude." He stared at Jerry, then threw the bits of paper on the sidewalk and walked away.

Tied up. Neatly.

I make myself available. I leave openings.

Contact. Contact is made. Good.

Advice is asked. Given. By the same person. Frequently myself. There are many layers.

I collect. I connect. What? That which counts. That which, in my opinion, counts. I discard, discount, disconnect. I judge. I interpret and clarify. I annotate. I am working on an annotated edition of—you name it.

Exploring interests me, I'm an explorer.

Natural phenomena interest me.

My height interests me. So do my eyes. How high am I? I'm curious. What is there left to tell you, my age?

Grow up.

I'm a thinker in the broad sense, I choose and gather. I collate. I'm a collater. I put together and form new patterns out of old shapes. It's my own peculiar sense of proportion, that's all I have to offer. I sign my own name.

I've just reread these pages. Words and words, lines of lines. I've just reread this fiction. There's an inconsistency of characterization, the characterization's uneven.

Enough. There are elements for a story here. If I were really Paul Friedman I'd write it.